The Girl from Scotland Yard

The Girl from Scotland Yard

Edgar Wallace

WILDSIDE PRESS

Originally published in 1926-27.

Published by Wildside Press LLC.
Visit us online at wildsidepress.com.

CHAPTER I.
AT TEA

As Lady Raytham drew aside the long velvet curtains, she looked down into Berkeley Square. It was half-past four o'clock on a cheerless February evening. Rain and sleet were falling and a thin yellow mist added to the gloom of the dying day. An interminable string of cars and taxicabs was turning toward Berkeley Street, their shining black roofs reflecting the glare of the overhead light that had just then hissed and spluttered to life.

She looked blankly toward the desolation of the gardens, a place of bare-limbed trees and shivering shrubs—stared, as though she expected to see some fog wraith take a definite and menacing shape and give tangible form to the shadows that menaced reason and life.

She was a woman of twenty-eight, straight and slim. Hers was the type of classical beauty which would defy the markings of age for the greater part of a lifetime. A fascinating face, calm, austere. Her eyes were a cold English gray. You might imagine her the patrician abbess of some great conventual establishment, or a lady of broad manors defending inexorably the stark castle of her lord against the enemy who came in his absence. Analyse her face, feature by feature, put one with the other, and judge her by the standards which profess to measure such things, and brow and chin said "purpose" with unmistakable emphasis.

She was not in her purposeful mood now; rather was she uncertain and irritable, the nearest emotions to fear that she knew.

She let the curtains fall back until they overlapped, and walked across to the fireplace, glancing at the tiny clock. The salon was half lit; the wall sconces were dark, but the big lamp on the table near the settee glowed brightly. This room bore evidence of money lavishly spent. The greater part of its furnishings would one day reach the museums of millionaire collectors; three pictures that hung upon the apple-green walls were earmarked for the National Gallery.

As she stood looking down into the fire, there was a gentle tap at the door, and the butler came in. He was a tall man, rather portly in his way; a man with double chin and an unlined face. He carried a small salver in his hand, a buff oblong in the centre.

Lady Raytham tore open the envelope. It was dated from Constantinople, and was from Raytham. She had been expecting the telegram all that afternoon. Raytham, of course, had changed his plans. In that sentence was epitomized his life and career. He was going on to Basra and thence to Bushire, to see the interstate oil wells, or the sites of them. He was expensively apologetic for two closely written sheets. If he could not return before April, would she go on to Cannes as she had arranged? He was "awfully sorry," he must have said that at least four times.

She read it again, folded the pink sheets and laid them on the table.

The butler was waiting, head slightly bent forward as though to catch her slightest whisper. She did not look at him.

"Thank you."

"Thank you, m'lady."

He was opening the door when she spoke.

"Druze, I am expecting the Princess Bellini and possibly Mrs. Gurden. I will have tea when they come."

"Very good, m'lady."

The door closed softly behind him. She raised her sombre eyes and looked at the polished wood of it with a curious, listening lift of her head as though she expected to hear something. But the butler was going slowly down the stairs, a quizzical smile in his eyes; his white, plump hands sliding in and over one another. He stopped on the landing to admire the little marble statue of Circe that his lordship had brought from Sicily. It was a habit of his to admire that Circe with the sly eyes and the beckoning finger. And as he looked, his mouth was puckered as though he were whistling.

A sharp rat-tat on the door made him withdraw from his contemplation. He reached the hall as the second footman opened the door.

Two women entered. Through the open door he had a glimpse of a limousine drawing away.

"Her ladyship is in the drawing room, your highness. Shall I take your highness's coat?"

"You can't," said the first and the bigger woman brusquely. "Help Mrs. Gurden out of hers. Why you wear such horrible contraptions I can't understand."

Mrs. Gurden smiled largely.

"Darling, I must wear something. Thank you, Druze."

Druze took the transparent silk coat and handed it to the second footman. The princess was already stamping up the stairs. She pushed open the door and walked in unannounced. Lady Raytham, standing by the fire, her head pillowed on her arm, looked up, startled.

"I'm so awfully sorry. Push the lights, Anita. The button is by your hand. Well?"

The Princess Anita Bellini struggled unaided out of her tweed coat and threw it over the back of a chair, jerked off her hat with another movement and tossed it after the coat.

People who saw Anita Bellini for the first time gazed at her in awe; there was a certain ruthless strength in every line, every feature. She was something more than fifty and was just under six feet in height.

The masculinity of the powerful face was emphasized by the gray hair, cut close in an Eton crop, and the rimless monocle which never left her eye. Between her white teeth she gripped a long amber holder in which a cigarette was burning.

Her speech was direct, abrupt, almost shocking in its frankness.

"Greta?"

She jerked the end of the cigarette holder toward the door.

"Being fussed over by Druze. That woman would ogle a dustman! She's that age. It is a horrible thing to have been pretty once and to have produced certain reactions. You can never believe that the spirit has evaporated."

Jane Raytham smiled.

"They say you were an awfully pretty girl, Nita—" she began.

"They lie," said Princess Anita calmly. "Russell's used to retouch my photographs till there was nothing left but the background."

Greta floated in, hands outstretched, her big red mouth opened ecstatically.

"Darling!" she burst forth, and caught both Jane's hands in hers. Anita Bellini's fleshy nose wrinkled in a sneer.

And yet she should have grown accustomed to Mrs. Gurden, for ecstasy was Greta's normal condition. She had that habit of touching people, holding them by the arms, stooping to look up into their faces with her big black eyes that sometimes squinted a little.

She had been pretty, but now her face was long and a little haggard, the face of a woman who was so afraid of missing something that she could not spare the time to sleep. Her lips were heavily carmined, her eyes carefully made up as though she were still expecting a call to return to the chorus from which Anita had rescued her.

"My lovely Jane! Exquisite as usual. That dress—don't tell me! Chenel—isn't it?"

"Is it?" Jane Raytham scarcely looked down. "No, I think it is a dress I bought in New York last year."

Greta shook her head speechlessly.

Anita Bellini blew out a smoke ring and tapped off the ash in the fireplace.

"Greta lays it on thick when she lays it at all," she said, and cast a critical eye over her hostess. "You're peaky, Jane. Missing your husband?"

"Terribly."

The irony of tone was not lost on Anita.

"Raytham—what is he doing? The man is ill of money and yet won't take a day off making it. Where the— Oh, here he is."

Druze wheeled in the tea wagon.

"Give me a whisky-and-soda, Druze, or I'll perish!"

She drank the contents of the goblet at a gulp and handed back the glass. She fixed her monocle more firmly and lit another cigarette. The door closed behind the butler.

"Druze wears well, Jane. Where did you get him?"

Lady Raytham looked up quickly.

"Does he? I scarcely notice him. He has always been the same as long as I can remember. He was with Lord Everreed before."

"That goes back a few years. I remember him when he was a young man."

The princess had an unhappy habit of smiling with her mouth closed. It was not very pretty.

"It is funny how age comes: thirty to fifty goes like a flash of lightning!"

She changed the subject abruptly and talked about her call of the afternoon.

"I went for bridge and got a string quartet playing every kind of music except one with a tune in it."

"It was lovely!" exclaimed Greta, her eyes screwed tight in an agony of admiration.

"It was rotten," retorted the gray-haired Anita. "And more rotten because my sister-in-law was there. The woman's narrowness depresses me."

Lady Raytham's eyes had returned to the fire.

"Oh!" she said.

"I asked her what she was going to do about Peter. Thank heavens she has a little sense there! Peter has been wiped off the slate. Margaret would not even discuss him. The only person who believed in him is Everreed, but Everreed was always a simpleton. He would never have prosecuted, but the bank forced his hand."

She said this with some satisfaction. She had never liked her nephew, and Peter hated her, hated her gibes at him when he, the son of a wealthy man, had preferred a private secretaryship with that great parliamentarian, Viscount Everreed, to entering his father's bank. She had sat in court with a contemptuous smile on her lips when the haggard boy had been sentenced for forging his employer's name to a check for five thousand pounds.

The woman by the fire stirred her tea absently.

"When does—"

"He come out? About now, I think. Let me see. He had seven years, and they tell me that these people get a remission of sentence for good conduct—three months in every year. Why, Heaven knows. We pay enormous sums to catch 'em, and as soon as they are safe under lock and key, we go tinkering with the lock to get them out."

"Disgraceful!" murmured Greta.

But Jane Raytham did not hear her.

"I wonder what he will do?" she mused. "Life will go pretty badly for a man like Peter—"

"Rubbish!" Anita snapped the word. "For goodness' sake don't get melancholy about Peter! He has been five years in prison; and at Dartmoor, or wherever he is, they teach men to use their hands to do something besides forge checks. He will probably make an excellent farm hand."

Lady Raytham shivered.

"Ugh! How awful!"

The princess smiled.

"Peter Dawlish is just a fool. He belongs to the type of humans that is made for other people's service. If you start worrying about Peter, you'll shed tears over the partridge that comes to your table! I wonder what he thinks about Druze?"

Lady Raytham looked up.

"Do you think he still hates him?"

Anita pursed her large lips.

"Druze was Everreed's butler and cashed the check; the next day Peter disappears on his holiday—in reality on his great adventure. He returns and is arrested, swears he knows nothing about the check, and accuses poor Druze of forgery—which doesn't save him from imprisonment."

Lady Raytham said nothing.

"Naturally Peter feels sore—if he was still right in believing Druze the villain of the piece. There may be trouble; we needn't deceive ourselves."

Her cigarette had gone out. She opened her bag with an impatient tug and searched.

"Matches? Never mind."

There was a letter in the bag; she tore a strip from the top and, bending, lit the paper at the fire.

"Who is Leslie Maughan?"

She was glancing at the signature which footed the letter.

"Leslie Maughan! I don't know him. Why?"

Anita crumpled the paper into a ball.

"Leslie Maughan would like to see me on a personal matter." Anita invented the stilted and supercilious accent which she supposed the writer of the letter might assume. "And Leslie Maughan will be glad to know what hour will be convenient for me to see him. He is an inventor or a borrower of money, or he has an expedition to the Cocos Islands that he would like me to finance. To the devil with Leslie Maughan!"

CHAPTER II.
THE GIRL DETECTIVE

Druze had come in noiselessly at the door and stood, hand clasping hand. His face was strangely pale; as he spoke, his right cheek twitched spasmodically.

"Yes?"

"Will your ladyship see Miss Leslie Maughan?"

"Miss!" exclaimed Anita, as Jane Raytham rose.

"Miss Leslie Maughan of the Criminal Investigation Department, Scotland Yard?"

Lady Raytham put out her hand and gripped the back of the chair; her face was bloodless; she opened her mouth to speak, but no word came. Greta was staring at the big woman, but Princess Anita Bellini had no eyes but for the pale butler.

"I will see her—in the small drawing room, Druze. Excuse me."

She swept out of the room and pulled the door behind her until Druze had disappeared round the lower landing. By her right hand was the door of her own room, and she entered swiftly and noiselessly, switching on the lights as she closed the door. She stared into the mirror. Ghastly! That white, drawn face of hers carried confession. Had she been betrayed? Had they fulfilled their threat?

Pulling out a drawer of her dressing table, she fumbled for and found a little pot of rouge and with a quick, deft hand brought an unaccustomed bloom to her cheeks.

Another glance at her face in the glass and she went out and sailed down the stairs, a smile on her lips, and in her heart despair.

All the lights were lit in the little drawing room, and her first emotion was one of surprise and relief. She had not known there were women detectives at Scotland Yard, but she could imagine them as hard-faced, sour creatures in ready-made clothes.

The girl who stood by the table looking down at the illustrated newspaper that Druze had supplied looked to be about twenty-two. She wore a straight nutria coat, a big bunch of violets pinned to one of the revers. She was as tall as Jane Raytham and as straight; trim silken ankles, neatly shod. The face under the upturned brim of a little felt hat was more surprising yet. A pair of dark eyes rose to meet Jane Raytham's. The lips red as Greta's, yet owing nothing to artifice, were finely moulded. She had a firm, round chin, and the hint of a white throat somewhere behind the protective fur. In some confusion Lady Raytham catalogued the visible qualities of her unexpected caller.

"You are not Miss Maughan?" she asked.

When Leslie Maughan smiled, she smiled with eyes and lips, and the dimpled hollows that came to her cheeks made her seem absurdly young.

"Yes, that is my name, Lady Raytham. I am awfully sorry to bother you, but my chief is rather a martinet."

"You are a detective? I didn't know—"

"That there were women detectives?" asked the girl. "And you're right! My position is unique. I am an assistant to Chief Inspector Coldwell. The commissioners, who are rather conservative people, do not object to that. But I suppose I really am a detective. I make inquiries."

She stood by the table, one hand on her hip, one playing with the leaves of the picture paper, her unwavering gaze fixed on Jane Raytham.

"I'm making inquiries now, Lady Raytham," she said quietly. "I want to know why you drew twenty thousand pounds from your bank last Monday."

For a second the woman was panic-stricken; so far lost control that she all but stammered the truth. The will that held her silent, apparently unmoved, was the supreme effort of her life. Then her training came to her rescue.

The control of her voice was perfect.

"Since when have the police had authority to supervise the banking accounts of private citizens?" she asked in cold, measured tones. "That is an extraordinary request! Is it then an offence for me to withdraw twenty thousand pounds from my own account? How did you know?"

"One gets to know things, Lady Raytham." She was cool, unruffled by the indignation, real or simulated. "Lady Raytham, you think we are being very impertinent and abominable. And it is certain that, if you report this matter to Scotland Yard, I shall be reprimanded. But we expect that—"

Jane Raytham had so far recovered toward the normal that she could open her gray eyes in astonishment.

"Then why on earth have you come?" she asked.

She saw Leslie Maughan draw a deep breath; the ghost of a smile trembled at the corner of her mouth and vanished.

"Twenty thousand pounds is a lot of money," she said softly. There was a note of pleading in her voice, and suddenly, with a cry she could not suppress, the significance of the visit flashed upon the woman. They knew. The police knew the destination or purpose of that money.

Her breath came faster; she could only look into those dark eyes in fear and try as best she could to order her thoughts. Dark eyes—violet, not the burned brown of Greta's, but a violet that was almost black. A detective—this slip of a girl! She was well dressed, too; the femininity in Jane Raytham took stock of it unconsciously. The gloves were from Renaud's; only Renaud cut that quaint, half-gauntlet wrist.

"Won't you tell me? It might save you so much unhappiness. We try to do that at the Yard—save people unhappiness. You'd never dream that, would you? But the police are more like big brothers than ogres. Won't you?"

Jane Raytham shook her head; it was a mistake, the only one she made, to attempt speech.

"No, I won't!" she said breathlessly. "There is nothing to tell. Your interference is unwarrantable. I shall write. I shall write."

She swayed, and instantly Leslie Maughan was by her side; and the strength of her grip was the second surprise that Jane Raytham had.

With an effort, she wrenched her arm free.

"Now you can go, please! And if I do not report you, it is because I think you have acted in ignorance—overzeal."

She nodded toward the door, and Leslie slowly gathered up her bag and her umbrella.

"If you ever want me, you will find my telephone number on my card."

Lady Raytham still held the crumpled card in her hand. Now she looked at it and very deliberately walked to the fire and dropped it into the flames.

"Or the telephone book," said Leslie, as she went out.

Druze was in the hall, dry-washing his hands with nervous rapidity. He hastened to the street door and opened it.

"Good-night, miss," he said huskily, and she looked at him and shivered. Why Leslie Maughan shivered she did not know, but she had at that moment a vivid and terrifying illusion.

It was as though she were looking into the blank eyes of one who was already dead.

CHAPTER III.
MEETING PETER

Leslie came striding briskly along the Thames Embankment. It was a bitterly cold night, and the nutria coat was not proof against the icy norther that was blowing. The man who walked by her side was head and shoulders taller than she. He had the gait of a soldier, and his umbrella twirled rhythmically to his pace.

"Suicide on the left," he said pleasantly, as though he were a guide pointing out the sights.

The girl checked her pace and looked back.

"Really? You don't mean that, Mr. Coldwell?"

Her eyes were fixed upon the dark figure sprawling across the parapet, his arms resting on the granite crown, his chin on his hands. He was a gaunt figure of a man, differing in no respect from the waifs who would gather here from midnight onward, and strive to snatch a little sleep between the policeman's visits.

"It is any odds," said Mr. Coldwell carefully, "when you see one of these birds watching the river in that way, he is thinking up a new way of settling old accounts. Are you interested—sentimentally?"

She hesitated.

"Yes, a little. I don't know whether it's sentiment or just feminine curiosity."

She left his side abruptly and walked back to the man, who may have been watching her out of the corner of his eyes, for he straightened himself up quickly.

"Down and out?" she asked, and heard his soft laugh.

"Down but not out," he replied, and it was the voice of an educated man, with just a trace of that drawl, the pleasant stigmata which the universities give to their children. "Did I arouse your compassion? I'm sorry. If you offer me money I shall be rather embarrassed. You will find plenty of poor beggars on this sidewalk who are more worthy objects of—charity. I use the word in its purest sense."

She looked at his face. A slight moustache and a ragged fringe of beard did not disguise his youth. Chief Inspector Coldwell, who had come closer, was watching him with professional interest.

"Would you like to know what I was really thinking about?" There was an odd quality of banter in his voice. "I was thinking about murder! There is a gentleman in this town who has made life rather difficult for me, and I had just decided to walk up to him at the earliest opportunity and pop three automatic bullets through his heart when you disturbed the homicidal current of my thoughts."

Coldwell chuckled.

"I thought I recognized you. You're Peter Dawlish," he said, and the shabby figure lifted his hat with mock politeness.

"Such is fame!" he said sardonically. "And you are Coldwell: the recognition is mutual! And now that I have hopelessly committed myself, I presume you will call the nearest city policeman and put me out of the way of all temptation."

"When did you come out?" asked Coldwell.

The girl listened, staggered. They had been discussing this man not a quarter of an hour before; she had spent the afternoon thinking of him; and now to meet him on that wind-swept pavement, he of all the millions of people in London, was something more than a coincidence. It was fatalistic.

"Mr. Dawlish, I wonder if you will believe me when I say that you're the one man in London I was anxious to meet. I only knew to-day that you were—out. Could you call and see me to-night?"

The man smiled.

"Invitations follow thick and fast," he murmured. "Only ten minutes ago I was asked into a Salvation Army shelter! Believe me, madam—"

"Mr. Dawlish"—her voice was very quiet, but very clear—"you are being awfully sorry for yourself, aren't you?"

She did not see the flush that came to his face.

"I suppose I am," he said, a little gruffly. "But a man is entitled—"

"A man is never entitled to be sorry for himself in any circumstances," she said. "Here is my card."

She had slipped back the cover of her bag, and he took the little pasteboard from her hand, and, bringing it close to his eyes, read, in the dim light that a distant lamp afforded:

Will you come and see me at half-past ten? I shan't offer you money; I won't even offer to find a job for you cutting wood or sorting waste paper. It is a very much bigger matter than that.

He read the name and subscription again, and his brows met.

"Oh, yes. Really—yes, if you wish."

He was, of a sudden, awkward and uncomfortable. The girl was quick to recognize the change in his manner and tone.

"I'm afraid I'm rather a scarecrow, but you won't mind that?"

"No," she said, and held out her hand.

He hesitated a second, then took it in his. She felt the hardness of the palm, and winced at the significance of it. In another second she had joined the waiting Coldwell. Peter Dawlish watched them until they were out of sight, and then, with a little grimace, turned and walked slowly toward Blackfriars.

"I knew about the smallness of the world," said Coldwell, swinging his umbrella, "but I had no idea that applied to London. Peter! It's years since I saw him last. He was rather a weed five years ago."

"Do you think he really is a forger?"

"A jury of his fellow countrymen convicted him," said Mr. Coldwell cautiously, "and juries are generally right. After all, he needed the money: his father was an old skinflint, and you cannot run a hectic establishment, and escort pretty ladies to New York, on two hundred and fifty pounds per annum. He was a fool; if he hadn't taken that three months' holiday the forgery would never have been discovered."

"Who was she?" Leslie asked; she felt that this question was called for.

"I don't know. The police *cher-chezed la femme*—forgive my mongrel French—but they never ran her to earth. Peter said it was a chorus girl from the Paris opera house. He wasn't particularly proud of it."

The girl sighed.

Near the dark entrance of Scotland Yard Mr. Coldwell stopped.

"Now," he said, standing squarely before her, "perhaps you will cease being mysterious, and tell me why you are so frantically interested in Peter Dawlish that you have talked Peter Dawlish for the past three days?"

She looked up at him steadily from under the lowered brim of her hat.

"Because I know just why Peter Dawlish wants to kill and whom he wants to kill!" she said.

"Druze! A child would guess that!" scoffed the detective. "And he wants to kill him because he thinks Druze's evidence sent him to jail."

She was smiling—a broad smile of conscious triumph.

"Wrong!" she said. "If Druze dies, it will be because he doesn't love children!"

Mr. Coldwell could only gape at her.

CHAPTER IV.
PETER'S LODGINGS

"Let me get this right," Coldwell said slowly. "Druze will be killed—if he is killed—because he does not like children?"

Leslie Maughan nodded.

"I know you hate mysteries. Everybody in Scotland Yard does," she said; "and one day I will tell you just what I mean. Do you remember last August you gave me a month's vacation?"

Chief Inspector Coldwell remembered that very well.

"I went to Cumberland just to loaf around," she said. "I was most anxious to pretend that there wasn't such a place in the world as Scotland Yard. But I've got that prowling, inquisitive spirit that would have made me the first woman inspector of the C.I.D. if the commissioners were not such stuffy, old-fashioned gentlemen! One day I was loafing through a little village, when I found something which brought me eventually to this conclusion, that Druze doesn't like children. And one day, when he discovers the fact, Peter Dawlish will kill him for it!"

"More mysterious than ever!" exclaimed Coldwell. "You're probably chasing a boojum. It is the fate of all enthusiastic young officers—not that you're an officer."

Leslie Maughan had started her police career as a very junior stenographer at Scotland Yard. Her father had been that famous Assistant Commissioner Maughan whose exploits have formed the basis for so many stories of police work, and he had left his daughter with an income which put her above the necessity of working for her living. But police investigation was in her blood, and she had graduated through successive stages, until the authorities, reluctant to admit that any woman had an executive position at police headquarters, admitted her to the designation of "assistant" to the chief of the Big Four.

"She's brilliant; there's no other word for her," he had told the chief com-missioner. "And although I don't think it's much of a woman's job, there never was a woman who was better fitted to hold down a high position at the Yard."

"What are her chief qualifications?" asked the commissioner, slightly amused.

"She thinks quick and she's lucky," was the comprehensive reply.

This question of luck exercised the mind of Leslie as she walked home to her flat in the Charing Cross Road. The very fact that that apartment was hers was strong support for the theory of luck. She had taken a long lease of a floor above a moving-picture house at a time when flats were going begging. She might have drawn double the rent from a subtenant; but the place was central, comparatively cheap, and she withstood all temptations to change her abode at a profit.

A side door led to the apartments, and she had hardly closed the door behind her when a voice hailed her from the top of the stairs.

"That you, Miss Maughan?"

"That's me," said Leslie.

She hung her coat in the narrow hall and went upstairs to the girl who was waiting on the landing. Lucretia Brown, her one servant, was a very tall, broad-shouldered girl, with a round and not unpleasant face. She stood now with her hands on her hips, surveying her mistress.

"I thought you were—" she began.

"You thought I'd been murdered and thrown into the river," said Leslie good-humouredly. "As you always think if I am not back on the tick!"

"I don't trust London," said Lucretia.

It was her real name, chosen by a misguided farm labourer, who, having heard a lecture on the Borgias, delivered at the parish hall, came away with a vague idea that the historical character who bore that name was a worthy creature.

"I never did trust London and I never will. Have you had dinner, miss?"

"Yes, I've had my dinner," said Leslie, and looked at the clock. "I am expect-ing a man to call here at half-past ten, so, when you open the door to him, please don't tell him that I'm out and not expected back for three weeks."

Lucretia made a little face.

"Half-past ten's a bit late for a gentleman visitor, miss. A friend of yours?"

Leslie could never train her out of a personal interest in her affairs. In a way Lucretia was privileged. Her first memory was of the broad-faced Lucretia pushing a perambulator in which Leslie took the air.

"Is it anybody we know, miss? Mr. Coldwell?"

Leslie shook her head.

"No," she said, "he is a man who has just come out of prison."

Lucretia closed her eyes and swayed.

"Good heavens!" she said in a hushed voice. "I never thought I'd live to see the day when you'd be having a convict up to see you at half-past ten at night! What about asking a policeman to stand by the door, miss?"

"You're much too partial to policemen," said Leslie severely, and the big maid grew incoherent in her indignant protests.

Half-past ten was striking from St. Martins-in-the-Fields when the door-bell rang, and Lucretia came in to her, eyes big with excitement.

"That's him!" she said melodramatically.

"Well, let him in."

"Whatever happens," began Lucretia, "I'm not responsible."

Leslie pointed to the door. He came so lightly up the stairs that she did not hear his steps. The door opened and Lucretia backed in.

"The gentleman," she said loudly, and cast an apprehensive glance at the stranger as she sidled out of the room and closed the door.

Peter Dawlish stood where Lucretia had left him, his soft hat in his hand, glancing from the girl to the cosy room, a smile on his thin face. She saw now how shabbily dressed he was: his shirt was collarless, his boots gray with mud, the old, ill-fitting suit he wore stained and patched.

"I warned you I was a scarecrow," he said, as though he read her thoughts. "They gave me a beautiful prison-made suit at Dartmoor, but it didn't seem the right kind of equipment with which to face a censorious world, so I swapped it for this."

She pushed a chair up to the fire.

"Sit down, won't you, Mr. Dawlish?"

" 'Mr. Dawlish,' " he repeated. "That sounds terribly respectable."

"You may smoke if you wish," she said, as he seated himself slowly, and again he smiled.

"I wish, but I have not the wherewithal." She hastily opened a drawer and took out a tin of cigarettes: "Thank you," he said.

He took the cigarette in his fingers and frowned.

"That is certainly queer," he said.

"What is certainly queer?" she asked.

"These gaspers; I used to smoke them in the old days. Had 'em imported from Cairo. You can't buy them here, at least you couldn't when I—retired. Heigho! Am I being very sorry for myself again? That stung! I loathe these self-pitiers, and it was a revelation to discover that I had gone over to the majority."

He lit the cigarette and drew luxuriously.

"This is rather wonderful," he said.

"Have you had any food?" she asked.

He nodded.

"I dined like a Sybarite, at a small shop in the Blackfriars Road. The dinner cost sixpence; it was rather an extravagance, but I felt I needed bracing for this ordeal."

"You have no lodging?"

He shook his head.

"No, I have no lodging."

He was twiddling his long, thin fingers. She noted with satisfaction that his hands were scrupulously clean, and again he seemed to divine her thoughts, for he looked down at them.

"I don't exactly know what information I can give you, if it is information you require, and if you had been a male-of-the-species policeman I should have declined your invitation rather loftily! But a woman policeman is unique. I've seen them, of course—rather fat little bodies with squat little helmets. I suppose they're useful."

He noticed that she herself was not smoking, and commented upon it.

"No, I very rarely smoke," she said. And then, in a changed tone: "Do you mind if I speak very plainly?"

"The plainer the better," he said, and he leaned back in his chair and sent a cloud of smoke to the ceiling.

"I dare say you'll be forced to walk London to-night?"

"It has become a habit," said Peter Dawlish. "And really, it would be rather amusing if one weren't so horribly tired. They gave me a little money when I left prison—not much. One gets quite a lot of sleep in the daytime, especially the sunny days, in odd corners of the parks. And on rainy nights I know a gardener's tool house, which is not perhaps to be compared with the bridal suite at an expensive hotel, but is cosy. I slept there last night with an ex-colonel of infantry and a lawyer who lived in the same ward at Dartmoor."

She eyed him steadily.

"To-night you will sleep decently," she said, in her quiet, even tone; "and to-morrow you will buy a new suit of clothes and interview your father."

He raised his eyebrows, amusement in his eyes.

"I didn't realize that you had scraped down to the family skeleton," he said. "And why am I to do this, Miss Maughan? The suit of clothes would be a waste of money; my parent would not be impressed by my appearance of affluence. Rather he would imagine that I had found another good-natured gentleman who trusted me with his check book. Furthermore, all this would cost money; and I think you should know, before we go any further, that I am not taking any money from you on any pretext."

She had the extraordinary knack of making him feel foolish. He always remembered afterward that in the first two meetings with this strange girl he had gone hot and cold either at her words or the inflection of her voice.

"That kind of pride which refuses to take money from a woman is very admirable." There was a note of cold sarcasm in her voice which made him writhe. "It is the attitude of mind behind man's subconscious sense of superiority to the female of the species! It is not particularly flattering to a woman, but it must be immensely gratifying to a man! May I ask you another question, Mr. Peter Dawlish? Do you intend sinking down into the dregs? Is your vista of life lined on either side by common lodging houses, with a pauper's graveyard at the end of it?"

"I don't exactly see what you're driving at."

She had made him angry and was secretly amused.

"I shall do my best, naturally, to find work. I had an idea of going abroad."

"Exactly." She nodded. "To one of the colonies. It is the most popular of all delusions that people without grit or ambition can magically acquire these qualities the moment they go ashore at Quebec or Sydney, or wherever their high spirits lead them."

He was laughing now in spite of himself.

"You've certainly got a knack of riling a man."

"Haven't I?" she put in. "I'll tell you what I was driving at, Mr. Dawlish. For you to refuse a loan of money now suggests that you're perfectly satisfied in your mind that you will never earn enough to repay the loan. The only way you can justify a refusal of money is to believe that you can never pay it back; that you're going to belong to the bread lines and the park benches and the public charities."

She saw that her shaft had got home, and went on quickly:

"Of course you will do nothing of the sort! You've come out of prison with a grievance against the world, and you're hardly to be blamed for that. I should imagine you are one of the few innocent men who ever went to Dartmoor."

He looked at her shrewdly.

"You believe I was innocent?"

She nodded.

"I'm pretty sure," she said, and then: "Do you carry a gun?"

He laughed aloud.

"The price of a Browning pistol would keep me in luxury for two months," he said. "No, I carry nothing more dangerous than a toothbrush."

The drawer from which she had taken the cigarettes was still open; she put in her hand and took out a small black cash box, and jerked back the lid.

"We will do this thing in a businesslike way," she said. "You will find a paper and pencil on the desk; sign an IOU for twenty pounds. If you believe in your heart of hearts that you'll be unable to pay me back, that a man of twenty-nine or twenty-eight, or whatever age you are, will never earn a sufficient margin above his cost of living to send back that money in a year or two years, then you need not take a cent. And this little bit of charity, as you call it—"

"I've called it nothing of the sort."

"In your mind you have," she said calmly. "It is very rude to contradict a lady! Now, Mr. Dawlish, I challenge you! If you think you are permanently down and out, the incident is finished, and I think you're finished, too."

She looked at him through her half-closed eyes, nodding slowly.

"You mean I'm not worth salving?" he asked, and got up. "I'll accept your challenge."

He took the pencil, scribbled a few words on the writing pad, and, tearing it off, handed it to the girl.

"Produce your twenty pounds."

He was amused in a sour way, but his anger was mostly directed inward to himself, that he should be angry at all. If anybody had told him, when he had walked into that room, that he would accept a loan of money from the girl who had not been absent from his thoughts since he had met her, he would have laughed at such a suggestion. Yet here he was, counting solemnly the notes as they were handed to him, and pocketing them without one single qualm of conscience.

"I think I'm beginning to know myself," he said. "I started a weakling, and prison hasn't improved me. No, no, I do not mean that it is a weakness to accept this money, but it would have been a weakness to refuse. I'm awfully obliged to you."

She held out her hand.

"Where will you be staying?" she asked.

"I don't know. But I will keep in touch with you. Please don't bother about me any more. If I can't get a job of some kind, I'm really not worth helping. Why are you doing this? It isn't part of the usual police procedure."

She shook her head.

"The police help where they can, you ought to know that," she said quietly. "But I admit that this is a purely personal action on my part. You are part of a big experiment. It isn't my womanly heart, but my scientific brain that is dictating just now." And then, going off at a tangent: "I wish you would shave yourself, Mr. Dawlish. You look too much like a musical genius to be thoroughly wholesome."

He was still chuckling to himself when Lucretia closed the outer door upon him with unnecessary violence.

He knew a small temperance hotel where he could sleep that night, a place in Lambeth, near Waterloo Station. "Temperance hotel" was rather a grand name for an establishment which was only a little superior to a common lodging house, but he guessed it was too late to get a bed at any of the Rowton houses.

He walked briskly down Charing Cross Road and into the Strand, crowded with cars and taxis, for the theatres were closing and the northern sidewalk was almost impassable. And then he thought he saw his mother preceding another lady into a car, and stopped. Yes, it was Margaret Dawlish, and the lady with the dirty-gray hair was Aunt Anita. He could afford to grin now, and the discovery was very pleasurable. He could well imagine that if he had seen that party earlier in the evening, the sight would have evoked a sneer and just that twinge of self-pity against which he was trying hard to guard himself.

He turned back, lest in passing they recognize him, and went down Villiers Street, mounting the stairs to Hungerford Bridge. It was not the twenty notes in his pocket, a compact, cosy little roll, that made his heart and his step lighter; he had caught something of the girl's spirit, had been imbued with a little of her courage and sanity.

Leslie Maughan puzzled him. She was more than pretty; there was in her face a spirituality which he had not detected in the face of any woman of his acquaintance or knowledge. He realized with a start that he had always disliked clever women. He liked them soft and feminine, and, if the truth be told, a little silly. But he liked this capable and pretty young woman.

Leslie Maughan had just enough of the official quality to keep him at a distance, and yet she was genuinely friendly, as friendly as a sensible elder sister might be, though in truth she must be years younger than he. Sometimes he felt a very old man; Leslie Maughan had made him feel like a child.

He was over the middle of the river now, and there was revealed to him the pageantry of the Embankment, with its lights reflected in the dark waters of the Thames. He felt himself responding to the glow and colour of it. And then, for no reason at all, he had an uncomfortable feeling that he could not trace, but instinctively he looked back. There were several people crossing with him, but immediately behind him, not half a dozen yards away, were three little men who moved shoulder to shoulder. They had the curious high-stepping walk which he had seen in Orientals, a sort of modified prance. They were not speaking to one another, as friends might who were walking home together, and, curiously enough, it was their silence which made him uneasy. Five years in a penal establishment had not been a good nerve cure for a man of Peter Dawlish's temperament.

He ran down the steps and found himself in a dim and gloomy street. From here was a short cut to the York Road, near where his temperance hotel was situated. His way led him through a deserted street of tiny houses, that was not quite a slum, but was barely respectable. As he turned into the thoroughfare, he glanced back and saw that the three little men were following. They moved noiselessly, as though they were wearing rubber shoes. Peter crossed the road and they followed a little nearer to him.

He was wondering whether it would not be better to turn and face them till they had passed. He had decided upon this action, when something fell over his head. He raised his hand quickly to catch at the thin rope, but it was too late. The slip knot tightened about his throat, two muscular little figures leaped at him, and in another second he was lying on the ground, fighting for life, strangled, his head bursting, his hands clawing at the rope. And then consciousness left him. After an eternity he felt somebody lifting him up and propping him against a wall; a brilliant light shone on his face.

Peter put his hand to his throat; the rope had gone, but he could still feel the deep depression it had made upon his skin.

"What was the game?" said a gruff voice.

He blinked up, could distinguish a helmeted head—a policeman.

"How do you feel? Would you like me to get an ambulance? I can put you into the hospital in a minute."

Shaking in every limb, Peter struggled to his feet.

"I'm all right," he said unsteadily. "Who were they?"

The policeman shook his head.

"I don't know. They passed me at the end of the street, and I thought they looked queer. Little fellows with flat noses; more like monkeys than men. And then I saw them go for you and came after them. I think I just about saved your life, young fellow."

"I think you did," said Peter ruefully, as he felt at his scarred throat.

"Run! I never saw anybody run as fast as they did," said the constable. "Did you have a row with them?"

"No, I never saw them before in my life," said Peter.

"Humph!" The officer was looking at him dubiously. "Wonder who they were? They talked in some lingo I didn't understand. I only caught one word, or maybe it's two—orange pander or bander."

"*Orang blanga?*" asked Peter quickly, and whistled.

"Know 'em?"

Peter shook his head.

"No, I don't know them. I guess their nationality. Javanese."

The officer was loath to leave him.

"Where are you going now?"

"I'm trying to find a lodging."

He was still far from recovered, for when he took a step the street and the officer went round in a mad whirl, and but for the policeman's arm he would have fallen.

"You'll get yourself pinched for being drunk," said the policeman humorously. "Lodgings? Now where did I see a lodging?"

He switched on his light, walked slowly down the street, flashing the lamp upon the windows. Presently he stopped.

"Here you are," he said.

Peter made a slow and cautious way to where the policeman was standing. The lantern was focused upon a little card in the window:

Lodgings for a Respectable Young Man.

"Will this do for you?"

Peter nodded, and the constable rapped gently on the door. He had to wait some time, but presently there was a heavy foot in the passage and a woman's voice asked hoarsely:

"It's all right, missis," said the custodian of the law. "I'm a policeman; there's a gentleman here who wants lodging."

The door was unlocked and opened a few inches.

"I've got a room, yes, but it's a bit late, ain't it?"

The constable uttered an exclamation of surprise.

"Why, bless me, it's Mrs. Inglethorne!"

"Yes, it's Mrs. Inglethorne," repeated the woman bitterly. "And well you ought to know, considering the trouble you police have brought on me! My old man being as innocent as a babe unborn, and our lodger as nice a young man as ever drew the breath of life!"

She peered at Peter in the reflection from the policeman's light; he saw a bloated red face, a loose mouth, and eyes of singular smallness. She was short and stout and wore a red flannel dressing gown, though apparently she had not disrobed for the night.

"I can't take you unless you've got money," she said. "I've been done before."

Peter skinned a pound from the roll and showed it to her.

"All right, come in," she said ungraciously.

Stopping only to thank the policeman for his help, Peter followed her into the narrow, evil-smelling passage, and the door closed behind him.

Fate had played its supreme joke on Peter Dawlish when it had led him to the unsavoury home of Mrs. Inglethorne.

She struck a match, lit a smelly little oil lamp, and preceded him up a steep, short flight of stairs to the floor above.

"Here's the room," she said, and he followed her into the front and the best bedroom in the house.

To his surprise, it was fairly well furnished: the bed was a new one, the walls had been lately papered; the two cheap engravings which constituted the pictorial embellishment of the apartment were in good taste.

"This was my lodger's room. He furnished it himself," said Mrs. Inglethorne rapidly. "As nice a man as ever drew the breath of life." She pronounced the last sentence so quickly that it almost seemed to be one word.

"Has he left you?"

She glanced at him suspiciously as though she thought that he was already informed as to the lodger's fate.

"He's got five years for busting a house up at Blackheath. My old man got seven, and an honester man there never was!"

A grim jest this, thought Peter Dawlish, that he, newly from that drab and drear establishment on Dartmoor, should be offered the vacant bedroom of one who had taken his place, was probably in the very cell in B Ward he had occupied.

"Pay in advance; eight shillings. I'll give you the change to-morrow." Mrs. Inglethorne held out her hand. In the light of the lamp she was even more unprepossessing than Peter had thought.

He gathered from certain evidence that prohibition would find no vigorous supporter in her. She took the money he gave her, and, setting down the lamp, opened a chest and extracted two new sheets. Evidently, thought Peter, as he watched the process of bed making, the burglar lodger was fastidious in the matter of comfort: the sheets were of linen. He discovered later that the pillows were of down, and that the bed itself was a luxurious article purchased at great cost in Tottenham Court Road.

"He liked everything of the best," said Mrs. Inglethorne, pausing in her labours to extol the absent tenant.

She went out soon after, leaving behind her a faint odour of spirituous liquor. He undressed slowly by the light of the lamp, preparing for the first good night's sleep he had had in a week.

The bed was soft, too soft. Although he was desperately tired, he tossed from side to side in a vain endeavour to sleep. It must have been two hours before he dozed, and then he woke.

It was a shrill, thin cry that woke him, and he sat up in bed, listening. It came again, from somewhere downstairs. It was a cat, he thought; no human voice was capable of such an attenuation of sound.

Again the cry! He got out of bed, walked to the door, opened it, and bent his head, listening. And then the hair of his head rose. It was a child's sobs he heard, and then a voice:

"I want my daddy! I want my daddy!"

He heard Mrs. Inglethorne's growling voice, as if she had been wakened from sleep.

"Shut up, blast you! If I get up to you I'll break your neck!"

And then the voices ceased, and Peter went back to bed. But it was not until the sound of closing doors in the street told him that the early workers were abroad, that he fell into a troubled sleep, disturbed by dreams of a child who cried and moaned all the time: "I want my daddy! I want my daddy!"

CHAPTER V.
A DEAD MAN

Leslie received a letter on the following afternoon, when she came back from her office.

104 Severall Street, Lambeth.

Dear Miss Maughan: I have lodgings at the above address, and in spite of the neighbourhood they are very comfortable, though my landlady is certainly the most unprepossessing female. There are six children in the house, ranging from a few months to a little girl of eight years. So, whatever are her faults, Mrs. Inglethorne—who drinks gin and has the fiery face of a Betsey Prig—has served her country most prolifically! I am buying some new clothes and hope to report, in a few days, that I am riding upward on a tide of prosperity.

What Mr. Coldwell called "The Dawlish Case," but which she thought about under quite another title, was completely occupying the girl's mind. It was her first big case in the sense that never before had the wheels of investigation moved of her own volition.

There had been more spectacular events with which she had been associated. She had helped Coldwell in the Kent Tunnel murder; it was her quick mind which had first grasped the fact that the principal informant of the police knew too much about the tragedy for one who had not participated in the crime. She it was who, searching the contents of a prisoner's pocket, had found the stain of indelible ink upon a silver coin, and had built upon that slender clue the theory which led to the arrest of the Flack Gang, and the capture of the plant with which they had been flooding Europe with forged one-thousand-franc notes.

She brought to police work the keenest of woman's wits and a queer instinct for ultimate causes that sometimes amazed and sometimes amused headquarters.

And now she was building up a new fabric, but, as she realized, on the shakiest of foundations—a little book of verse found in a Cumberland cottage.

She took it down from her shelf, a thin volume of Elizabeth Browning's poems. On the flyleaf was an inscription and eight lines of writing in a neat hand. A stanza of free verse, and not especially good free verse. She read it for the fiftieth time:

> *Do you recall*
> *One dusky night in June*
> *Over by Harrow Copse,*
> *Heart of my heart?*
> *Ecstasy lay on your lips,*
> *Nectar of gods was your gift—*
> *All in "the kiss of one girl"*
> *Joy and despair.*

The writer was no poet. Even as a writer of *vers libre* his effort left something to be desired.

She put away the book, returned to her desk, and sat for half an hour, her chin in her hands, her eyes fixed vacantly on the opposite wall. For the moment Peter Dawlish was off her hands, and though he came back again and again to her thoughts, it was not in the rôle of a responsibility.

She took from a drawer the tin of cigarettes she had offered him on the previous night, and examined it absently. She had searched London for this brand of Egyptian cigarettes, and in the end had found them in the last place in the world she expected—Scotland Yard. The chief commissioner, an old Egyptian officer, imported them for his own use.

She closed the lid, found an envelope, and addressing it to "Peter Dawlish, Esq., 104 Severall Street, London," she inclosed the cigarettes. It was nearly dark when Lucretia brought in her tea.

"You're not going out again to-night, miss, are you?" When Leslie replied in the affirmative: "What about taking me with you, Miss Leslie?"

Leslie did not laugh.

"Somehow I can't see you in the setting of a night club, Lucretia," she said.

"I could stay outside," insisted Lucretia stoutly. "Anyway, I'd never dream of going into a night club after what the papers say about 'em. I saw a party getting out of a car the other night—ladies! Why, miss, I could have carried all their dresses in a little bag! Disgraceful, I call it!"

Leslie laughed quietly.

"You've got to understand, Lucretia," she said, "that no woman is properly dressed for dinner unless she feels comfortably nude. Don't faint!"

"Women are not what they was," said Lucretia severely.

"That's the devil of it, Lucretia. They are!" said Leslie.

She had only half made up her mind as to the course she should pursue. Mr. Coldwell often twitted her about her luck, but her "luck" was largely a matter of abnormal instinct, and it was in her bones that there was tragedy in the air. Suppose she saw Lady Raytham again, and this time spoke not in parables, but in plain English? It required no particular effort on Leslie's part, for her moral equipment was free from the faintest tinge of cowardice. She had inquired that morning as to whether Lady Raytham had carried her threat into execution and had written to the chief commissioner, but apparently her ladyship had reconsidered her decision. Had Peter Dawlish told her of the attack which had been made upon him, and which had so surprisingly led him to Mrs. Inglethorne, she would have called at Berkeley Square before then. But Peter had been silent on the subject, and Leslie did not know till the next day of that surprising outrage.

She went to her bedroom and changed her dress; she was dining that night with Mr. Coldwell at the Ambassadors, which is sometimes called a night club by the uninitiated, but is in reality the centre of London's smart life. Over her flimsy gown, which Lucretia never saw without closing her eyes in mental anguish, she put on her heavy fur coat, slipped a pair of rubbers over her shoes, and sent Lucretia down for a taxi. At a quarter past seven she was pressing the visitors' bell at No. 377 Berkeley Square. The door was opened almost instantly by a footman.

"Have you an appointment with her ladyship?" he asked, as he closed the door upon her.

"No, she hasn't an appointment with her ladyship."

Leslie turned in amazement at the sound of a loud, raucous voice. It was Druze, who had come into the hall from a door beneath the stairs. The white face was red and blotchy; his hair untidy; there was a stain on his white shirt front, and when he walked toward her his step was unsteady. He was, in point of fact, rather drunk, and Mr. Druze drunk was an exceedingly different person from Mr. Druze sober.

The whole character of the man seemed to have changed. From being a shrinking, rather fearful servitor, he had become a blustering, loud-mouthed bully of a man.

"You can get out. Go on! We don't want you!"

He advanced toward her threateningly, but the girl did not move. The second footman had withdrawn to a respectful distance and was looking with frowning amusement at the antics of his chief.

"Do you hear what I say? Clear out! We don't want any spying police girls round here."

It looked as though he would use physical force to eject her, but his hand had hardly been raised when she said something in a low voice—one word. The big white hand went down; the blotchy red went out of his face, and he blinked at her like a man who was trying to swallow something that would not be swallowed. And then, looking up, she saw a resplendent figure at the head of the stairs. It was Lady Raytham.

"Come up, please."

The voice was hard and metallic. There was neither cordiality nor welcome in it, nor did Leslie expect any such demonstration. She mounted the stairs, but before she could reach the landing Lady Raytham had turned and preceded her into the drawing room. As she went in, she saw that her unwilling hostess was not alone. Before the fire stood a figure which was not wholly unfamiliar—a square, tall, Eton-cropped figure with a monocle, which fixed her with a keen and penetrating glance.

The contrast between the two women was startling. Lady Raytham had never looked more lovely, more fragile, Leslie thought, than she did at that moment. She also was going out to dinner, and she wore a dress of old gold, and about her neck a magnificent chain of emeralds that terminated in a square emerald pendant which must have been worth a fortune. Anita Bellini was in scarlet, a hard, shrieking scarlet that no other woman could have worn. And yet, for some remarkable reason, it suited her. The *godet* was of silver lace, decorated by big green and red stones and the thick jade bracelets and ruby necklet gave her an air of barbaric splendour.

"I am sorry you came, Miss Maughan; it is doubly unfortunate. If Druze had been normal, I should have sent you away without seeing you. As it is, I feel that at least an apology is due to you for the disgraceful condition of my servant."

Leslie inclined her head slightly. What she had to say could not be told before this big, steely-eyed woman who stood with her back to the fire, the inevitable cigarette between her lips, the shining eyeglass fixed upon the visitor.

"I wanted to see you alone if I could, Lady Raytham."

Jane Raytham shook her head.

"There is nothing you can tell me that I should not wish Princess Bellini to hear," she said.

Without turning her head, Anita flicked her cigarette ash into the fireplace.

"Perhaps Miss Maughan doesn't wish to speak before a witness," she said, in her hard, deep voice. "If I were Lady Raytham I should have reported you last night to your superiors and had you kicked out of Scotland Yard!"

Leslie smiled faintly.

"If you were Lady Raytham, there are so many things you would do, Princess," she said, "and there would be so many things that it would be quite unnecessary for you to do!"

Anita's eyes did not waver.

"Such as—" she suggested.

If she expected to frighten the younger woman she must have been disappointed. Leslie's lips were curved in a fixed smile.

"We have now come to the point," she said good-humouredly, "where I should not like to speak before witnesses, either—though some day I may speak before more witnesses than you can crowd into a room twice this size; as many, Princess, as can squeeze themselves into Court No. 1 at the Old Bailey."

She said this without raising her voice, and now for the first time Anita Bellini gave the slightest hint of her emotion. The eyeglass dropped and was caught deftly and replaced with too-elaborate care. The strong mouth drooped a little, but recovered at once.

"That sounds almost like a threat to me," she said harshly. "Young lady, I think you're going to lose a job."

Quick as a flash came the answer:

"Before I lose my job, Princess, you will lose a very profitable source of income."

She did not wait for the answer, but turned to Lady Raytham.

"Will you see me alone, Lady Raytham?"

Jane Raytham's voice shook a little; she was a very bewildered woman.

"I brought you here to apologize to you for Druze," she said breathlessly, "and you have made use of the opportunity to insult my friend—a lady who—"

Her voice grew husky and she stopped as though she could not articulate further.

There was nothing more to be gained here, unless she was prepared to blurt her questions before the very woman who she was anxious should remain in ignorance of the information which had come to her. Leslie had unfastened her coat in coming upstairs; behind her brown fur Lady Raytham saw the silk-clad figure in mauve. Princess Anita Bellini smiled. She had a flair for Paris models.

"They pay you well in the police, my young friend," she said bluntly. "Who is the lucky gentleman who pays for your clothes?"

"My lawyer until I am twenty-five," said Leslie.

"Fortunate lawyer! Who is he?"

Leslie smiled.

"You ought to know him. He acted for you in your bankruptcy."

And with that parting shot she went out of the room, knowing she was a cat, but realizing that a cat was entitled to what pleasure she might find in getting under the skin of a tigress.

Half an hour later, Mr. Coldwell unfolded his serviette and shook his head soberly.

"You *are* a cat, too! But you're a clever little cat; and when, Tabitha, did you discover that her highness was a bankrupt? I confess that is news to me."

The girl laughed ruefully.

"I read gazettes," she said. "It is depraved in me, but I find them more interesting than the best sex novel that any school girl has ever written! The bankruptcy was arranged ten years ago in the quietest way. The princess took up her residence in a small country town before she filed her petition, and it is easy to keep these country proceedings out of the London papers. On this occasion she described herself as Mrs. Bellini. There is no law compelling you to use a foreign title."

"Pussy cat, pussy cat," murmured Mr. Coldwell. "And did she annihilate you?"

"She was slightly withering," said Leslie carelessly. "But Druze dropped! I'm awfully worried about that."

"I don't see why you should be," said Coldwell, and beckoned a waiter.

When the man had taken the order:

"Do you know, you're almost persuading me that there is something big behind this Dawlish mystery? I don't mean the discovery, which is very unlikely to be made, that Druze was the forger after all."

A tall woman had come into the restaurant and was glaring round through the thick lenses of her horn-rimmed spectacles. She was very straight and spare, her head covered with a mop of white hair, which lent her an almost comical air of ferocity. She nodded curtly to the inspector and went to meet the gesticulating maître d'hôtel.

"That is mamma," said Coldwell.

"Mamma? Whose mamma?"

"Your interesting convict's."

"Margaret Dawlish?" Leslie opened her eyes in astonishment. "This is the last place I should have expected to see her."

"She dines here every night," said Coldwell. "I have a good idea why."

Leslie looked at Peter's mother again; the square jaw, the thin lips, the deep eyes, all fulfilled the mental picture she had made of her.

"If you weren't here, do you know what I should do?" she asked at last.

"Whatever it is, don't!" said Coldwell apprehensively.

His relationship with Leslie was a curious one. In the old days of Commissioner Maughan he had been the colonel's chief assistant; though he was only a sergeant in those days, he was admitted very largely to the confidence of that genius of Scotland Yard; spent long week-ends at Sutton Cawley, and had assumed a sort of guardianship toward Colonel Maughan's motherless child. There never was a time within Leslie's recollection that Josiah Coldwell had not figured largely in her life. He was one of her father's executors, the best trusted of all his friends, and it was only natural, when she conceived the idea of adopting police work as a profession, that he should be her sponsor.

It was not until a very long time after she had put the suggestion to him that he agreed. At first he had pooh-poohed, then he had grown solemn, and then mournful; but in the end she had had her way.

"If you don't put me there, Uncle Josiah, I shall go into training as a private detective!"

It only needed this threat to force his capitulation, for private detectives were contemptible figures in the eyes of this regular policeman. For him it was a matter of pride that she had succeeded. To-day, if the truth be told, if she had expressed the slightest hint of weariness and a desire to return to the obscurity of what is termed "civilian life," he would have been thrust in the deeps of gloom.

He did not tell her this in the course of the dinner. She had guessed it easily enough long before, but he did venture to return to a matter which rather worried him. As the band struck up a dance tune and she rose invitingly, he groaned and came to his feet.

"I'll be awfully glad, Leslie, when you find a young man to dance these infernal jazzes with you. How can you expect the high-class crooks of London to have any respect for a man who dances in public?"

He was over sixty, yet, in truth, no better dancer took the floor that night. But it pleased him to talk of his decrepitude.

"I'm not made right," said Leslie, as he guided her through the dancers who crowded the floor. "Young men have no appeal for me whatever."

Mr. Coldwell peered down at her.

"Are you going to be one of those love-is-not-for-me girls?" he asked gloomily. "Somehow I can't imagine you running a garage of toy poms."

Leslie's eyes roved around the room, and presently they rested upon Margaret Dawlish; hard-faced, inflexible, the type of Roman mother who could never forgive the humiliation that Peter had brought upon her. How queer was the average man's conception of the average woman! The conventional mother, soft, yielding, ready to endure all and forgive all for the sake of her children, was no figment of imagination, but the throw-outs were innumerable. Leslie started to count all the instances she knew, and grew tired of the exercise. She had witnessed, incredible though it might seem, a mother dancing on this very floor while her child was dying in a nursing home a few streets away.

She knew mothers who could not speak of their daughters without growing incoherent with rage. And this was the fourth instance of a mother who could sweep her only son out of memory, out of existence, for some offence he had committed, not against her, but against society. Margaret Dawlish sat alone at a little table, very upright, very forbidding, and when the maître d'hôtel, in the manner of his kind, approached her with a smile, she dismissed him with a few words, and, raising her lorgnette, made an inspection of the dancers.

"That woman is granite," said Leslie, as the band stopped and they walked back to their table.

"Which? You mean Mrs. Dawlish? Yes. I rather think she is on the hard side. That sort of thing meant a lot to her. She hates this company and this place, but for five years, ever since her son was sent to prison, she has made a point of dining here."

Leslie nodded.

"A gesture of defiance! Gosh! These respectable people! They dare not leave a room for fear somebody talks behind their backs!"

It was toward eleven o'clock, and Coldwell had summoned the waiter to pay his bill, when a footman came from the vestibule and, bending over, whispered something to him.

"A phone message; I expect it's from the Embankment," he said. "Excuse me, Leslie."

He threaded a way through the dancers on the floor, and was gone ten minutes. When he came back, she saw his white eyebrows were met in a frown.

"The Kingston police think they've got a line to those infernal motor-car bandits," he said.

He referred to a gang which was occupying the public attention at that time—three men who, in hired or stolen motor cars, had been travelling through Surrey, holding up isolated residences at the point of a pistol, and getting away with as much portable property as they could lay their hands upon.

"I'll see you home," he said as he paid the bill, "and then I'll toddle down to Kingston. I wish to heaven the Kingston police would make their discoveries at a reasonable hour."

"I'll go with you," she said. "I'm not a bit sleepy, and it's a braw bricht moonlicht nicht!"

He looked at her dubiously.

"I don't know that you're dressed for a motor-car journey, but if you wish you can come along. I have phoned for the police car; it will be here in a few minutes."

She went out into the lobby to put on the woollen spencer she had brought in preparation for a cold journey home, and over that her coat. It was true that she never felt less like sleep; in a sense, she was at a loose end, and the prospect of doing a little work before she went to bed was a pleasing one, though in all probability she would play no other part than that of spectator and audience.

The trip promised to be the more interesting, because she had, that day, been tracing the previous convictions of three men who were suspected of being the motor bandits—and very commonplace individuals they were. That had been the most shocking discovery she made when she came to Scotland Yard—the commonplaceness, indeed the insignificance, of what it described as the criminal class. Out-of-work plumbers, labourers, carters, and clerks, with a painter here and there, formed the bulk of them. The women only had an individuality. There was no habitual woman criminal quite untouched by romance; their stories were altogether different, their lives more varied, and, if the truth be told, their enterprise and inventive qualities more fascinating.

She passed through the swing doors into the street. The night was bitterly cold and the sky overhead was clear. The bright moon which she had recklessly inferred was not in evidence, but there were all the other attractive conditions for a midnight ride.

The car was an open tourer with a plenitude of rugs, and as Mr. Coldwell fixed the rear screen to shield her face from the cutting air, the journey promised no discomforts. The car passed swiftly through Kensington and across Hammersmith Bridge, and in an incredibly short space of time was running down Kingston Vale. The driver pulled up at the police station behind a big touring car which was unattended, and they got down.

In the charge room they found the inspector talking to a middle-aged man who was apparently the owner of the car.

"Sorry to bring you down, Mr. Coldwell," said the inspector, "but this sounds almost like one of the motor crowd's little jokes."

The car owner apparently was the proprietor of a small garage. That afternoon he had been approached by a seemingly decent man, who asked him if he would come to London with the idea of negotiating for an important journey. The garage keeper, as it happened, had some business in town and had met the hirer at a little restaurant in the Brompton Road.

"He seemed all right to me," the garage keeper continued his narrative. "It was only after I got home that I began to smell a rat. He wanted me to pick him up at the end of Barnes Common, near the Wimbledon Road, at a quarter past ten to-night, and drive him to Southampton. He asked for a closed car, but I told him I hadn't got one that could do the journey, and I didn't like the idea, anyway. But as he offered me double the fare I should have asked, and paid half of it down, I agreed."

"Did you ask him why he wanted to go to Southampton at a quarter past ten?"

"That was the first question I asked," said the man. "He told me he was dining with some friends, and that that would mean he would lose the boat train—the *Berengaria* pulls out at five o'clock to-morrow morning, and all the passengers must be on the ship overnight. I've had that job before, so it wasn't unusual. The only queer thing about it was that, instead of asking me to pick him up at a house, he fixed this place on Barnes Common. But he told me he didn't want his friends to know that he was leaving the next day. At any rate, I fell for him, but as time went on I began to get suspicious and communicated with the police."

"What sort of looking man was he?" asked Leslie.

"A middle-aged man, miss," said the chauffeur-owner, a little surprised at a question from this quarter. "It struck me that he'd been booz—drinking a little, but that's neither here nor there. He was well dressed, and that's all I can tell you about him except that he was clean-shaven, had rather a big face, and wore a soft felt hat."

Coldwell turned to the girl.

"Does that describe any of the people we have been looking over?" he asked.

She shook her head.

"No," she said quietly, "but it rather accurately describes Druze!"

"Druze?" he said incredulously. "You're not suggesting that Druze is one of the gang?"

"I'm not suggesting anything," she said, biting her lip thoughtfully. "Did you notice his hands, Mr.—"

"Porter," said the chauffeur. "Yes, miss, I did notice his hands when he took off his gloves to pay me. They were very white."

She looked at Coldwell.

"That is an even more accurate description," she said.

"You didn't go to the Common, did you?" asked Coldwell.

"No, sir. The inspector went up in my car with a couple of policemen."

"He must have smelled a rat," said the local inspector. "There was no sign of anybody at a quarter past ten, and apparently he was very particular about his being there absolutely on time. He told Mr. Porter: 'If I'm not there by twenty-five minutes past, don't wait for me.' That sounds rather like the gang, Mr. Coldwell," he added. "It is an old trick of theirs to hire a car and arrange to be picked up in some quiet spot—"

The telephone bell tinkled in another room and he went to the instrument. He was gone five minutes. When he came back:

"The gang 'busted' a house the other side of Guilford at nine o'clock," he said. "The car smashed into a ditch and two of them have been caught by the Surrey police."

Coldwell pursed his lips.

"That disposes of your theory," he said.

Driving back up Kingston Vale, Coldwell expatiated upon his favourite theme, which might be headed, "No effort is wasted when you're dealing with law-breakers."

"A lot of men would grouse about being brought out in the middle of the night on a fool's errand, but it isn't possible to investigate the reason why a condensed milk tin has been found in an ashpit without learning something valuable. And if that hirer was friend Druze——"

"As it was," said Leslie promptly.

"Well, we've learned something," continued Coldwell. "It brings him into a new list, so to speak. He's in the people-who-do-strange-things class, and that makes him stand out from the mass of law-abiding citizens."

They passed swiftly down Roehampton Lane, climbed the little slope that carried them over the railway bridge, and had reached the middle of the Common when Chief Inspector Coldwell began to enlarge and illustrate his theory. Just ahead of them, Leslie saw the rear lights of a car moving out from the side of the road.

"Never despise little cases," he began, "because——"

There was a grinding of brakes; the car stopped so violently that Leslie's nose touched the glass screen painfully.

"What's wrong?" asked Coldwell sharply. He, too, had seen the car ahead, and his first thought was that his driver was avoiding a collision.

The police chauffeur was looking round.

"I'm sorry, sir, I was rather startled. Did you see a man lying on the side-walk?"

"No, where?" asked the interested Coldwell.

The driver reversed and the car moved slowly backward. They saw a black something in the darkness, and then, as the machine moved back a few more feet, the headlamps showed the figure of a man.

Coldwell got down from the car slowly.

"It looks like a drunk," he mumbled. "You'd better stay where you are, Leslie."

But his foot had hardly touched the ground before she had followed.

Well enough Inspector Coldwell knew that this was no drunk. The attitude, the outstretched arms, the legs slightly doubled, told him, before he saw the little pool of crimson on the sidewalk, that there was no life here.

For a second the two stood gazing down at the pitiable figure.

"Druze," said the girl quietly. "Somehow I expected it."

It was Druze, and he was dead. The heavy overcoat was buttoned across his chest; there was no sign of a hat, and his hands, ungloved, were tightly clenched. As she looked, Leslie saw a queer green glitter in the light of the motor lamps.

"He has something in his left hand," she said in a hushed voice, and, kneeling down, Inspector Coldwell pried loose the fingers, and the thing that the dead man held fell with a tinkle to the gravelled path.

Coldwell picked it up and examined it curiously. It was a large, square emerald in a platinum setting, one edge of which was broken, as though it had been torn forcibly from a large ornament.

"That is queer," he said.

She took the emerald from his hand and carried it nearer to the lamp. Now she knew that she had made no mistake. It was the pendant on the chain she had seen that evening glittering on Lady Raytham's neck!

CHAPTER VI.
THE EFFECT ON LADY RAYTHAM

In a few words she told her companion. For his part he was too worried about her presence to comprehend fully.

"You had better get into the car, Leslie. Driver, take Miss Maughan—"

"I'll stay here," said Leslie in a low voice. "I'm not very shocked. And please don't touch that overcoat."

He was stooping to unfasten the button when she spoke.

"Not till you let me see it."

Mr. Coldwell hesitated a moment and then stepped aside, and the girl bent over the figure, keeping her eyes averted from that white face.

"I thought so," she said. "The second button has been fastened to the third buttonhole. Whoever killed him, put on his overcoat and buttoned it. Now you can unfasten it."

Mr. Coldwell sent the chauffeur for assistance and resumed his examination of the body. The man had been shot at close range through the heart; the waistcoat had been burned by the explosion. There were no other injuries that he could see. One side of the figure was yellow with dust, as though it had been dragged some distance along the ground.

"I wish you wouldn't—"

Coldwell looked round in helpless distress. He had taken an electric flash light from the car before he sent it away, and this he had placed on the path so that the rays spread fan-shape over the body.

"Couldn't you wait at a little distance?"

"Please don't worry about me, Mr. Coldwell," said Leslie. There was no tremor in her voice, he noted with satisfaction. "I am not going to faint. You seem to forget that the majority of nurses are women; and death isn't so horrible to me as some expressions of life. Can I help you at all? I've got a tiny little pencil lamp in my bag."

He scratched his chin.

"I don't know," he said dubiously. "You might look in the road and see if you can find any marks of a body being dragged, and then search around a bit."

She got out the lamp, which, in spite of its smallness, gave a very bright light, and carried out his instructions methodically. She had not to look far before she found the traces she sought: a serpentine smear that reached from the centre of the road to the sidewalk. There were stains—little red smudges that were still wet when she put her finger to them.

The conditions were favourable to an undisturbed search, for Barnes Common was unusually free from traffic. One motor bus lumbered past, a homeward-bound limousine from town was succeeded by another, and if the chauffeurs were interested in the spectacle of a man kneeling by what looked like a heap of rags on the sidewalk, the occupants of the cars did not apparently share their curiosity.

She paced the trail, judged it to be between twelve and thirteen feet from the place where the body was found. On the other side of the footpath was rough, common land: grass and bushes in irregular patches. She began to search the ground; and here she had an unusual reward, for, passing round a thick, low bush, she saw, lying together on the grass, a number of objects. The first was a flat pocketbook that had been opened and its contents pulled out, for round about was a litter of papers, which she collected quickly. Fortunately, it was a still night, and there was no wind to carry them away. The second package was a brown envelope, and she made a brief examination.

There was a steamship ticket issued to "Anthony Druze, First Class Saloon, Southampton to New York." In this envelope was a new passport. The third object was also a pocketbook—brand-new—the perfume of the Russian-leather cover told her that. This also had been opened in such a hurry that the strap about it had been broken. It was stuffed tight with thousand-dollar notes.

She collected the three packages and sought for more, but there was none. And then she took stock of the place where she had found them. It was immediately behind a big bush which effectively screened all view of the road. She put her lamp close to the ground and moved it slowly. Here was a curiously mottled patch of grass; in some places it was gray with frost, in others wet and crushed. The ground was too hard for footprints, but without their aid she could reconstruct all that had happened here less than an hour ago. Somebody had come behind this brush to examine the contents of the pockets; the papers had been taken out one by one, examined and thrown away, and the object had not been robbery. The tightly filled pocketbook proved that. It could not have been a chance thief who came upon the body;

no honest person would have made this search. It had been somebody looking for a definite thing.

She went back to Coldwell with her discoveries just as the police car came flying over the railway bridge, followed by a motor ambulance. She told Coldwell hurriedly what she had found, and he was not surprised.

"I've been searching his pockets; most of them are inside out," he said. And then, abruptly: "Where is Peter Dawlish?"

She stared at him open-mouthed.

"Peter Dawlish? What has he got to do—"

And then she remembered Peter's threat, and saw that it was inevitable that suspicion should attach to him.

"He hadn't a pistol yesterday," she said, "and I doubt whether he's got one now. If Druze had been shot dead in the street I should think he'd be under suspicion, but Peter Dawlish would hardly shoot a man, put him in a car, and drive him to Barnes."

The old man nodded.

"I agree with you, Leslie, but we shall have to pull him in and make inquiries. Druze has been shot three times; that's rather a queer thing, and he has been shot through the heart! We shan't know exactly until the pathologist has seen him, but I think I am right. And listen, did you see the footprints?"

He pointed to the smooth granite curb, and she saw for the first time the indubitable impressions of a bare foot; the ball of the foot and toe prints were unmistakable.

He put the three packages Leslie had found in his overcoat pocket.

"Go along and see Lady Raytham and tell her what has happened. Take this with you, and for the love of Mike don't lose it!"

He put the square emerald in her hand, and she dropped it into her bag.

"If it's the pendant, as you say, find out what has happened to the rest of the necklace."

He bundled her into the police car, and she was glad to escape, because by now the large force of police on the spot had been augmented by that curious crowd which sooner or later gathers from nowhere on the scene of any tragedy.

The windows were in darkness when she drove up to the house in Berkeley Square, and instead of ringing she wielded the heavy knocker. She had to wait a little time, and then it was a footman who opened the door, and his manner and mien were both respectful and a little nervous.

"Do you want to see her ladyship, miss?" he said. "She's upstairs with Mrs. Gurden; there is Mrs. Gurden now."

Greta was coming down the stairs. She was in that peculiar style of evening dress which she affected. Greta made most of her own clothes from the latest Paris models and usually in the most unsuitable material. Their "home-madeness" was never blatant. They did not proclaim but hinted it.

Leslie looked up at the rouged face and the black, staring eyes, and it required no particular acumen on her part to detect Greta Gurden's agitation.

"Oh, my dear Miss whatever-your-name is," she said, "do come up and see Lady Raytham! You are Miss what-is-your-name? Maughan, isn't it? I'm so glad! Druze has been a perfect beast." She held out her hand dramatically; it was shaking. "You don't know how glad I am to see you."

Her eyelids were blinking up and down with a rapidity that fascinated and would have amused Leslie in any other circumstances.

"What has Druze been doing?" she asked.

"Won't you come up and see Lady Raytham?" begged Greta. "She'll tell you so much better than I. My dear Jane can put everything into the most understandable terms. Druze has been simply awful: made a terrible scene and walked out quite suddenly. It's dreadful what servants are coming to, isn't it? I think it must be the war or—"

A cool voice from the darkness above interrupted her flow of disjointed explanation.

"Ask Miss Maughan to come up. I want to see her—alone."

Leslie went up the stairs, and as she reached the first turn, she saw that the drawing-room door was open. There was no light on the stairs, save for that which came from the open door. In one corner of the spacious landing she saw a small-wheeled table.

She walked in, closing the door behind her. Lady Raytham was standing behind a little table near the fireplace. She wore a dark day dress without ornamentation, and Leslie's quick woman's eyes saw that she had changed her stockings; the very fine-textured, flesh-coloured hosiery she had seen on her earlier that evening had been replaced by a slightly darker pair. But only for a second did the details of the dress interest her. What a change had come to Jane Raytham's face! She was made up, that was clear. The delicate flush of her cheeks was neither natural nor normal in her; she had helped her lips toward a verisimilitude to a healthy red. Her eyes, however, defied all artificial aid; they seemed to have sunk into her head; great dark circles, which even careful powdering could not disguise, surrounded them.

"Have you brought me any news?" she drawled out. It was not like Lady Raytham to drawl. "I telephoned to you about an hour ago, but unfortunately

I could not catch you. On the whole, I think I prefer that a woman officer should deal with this case."

"Has he stolen anything?" asked Leslie bluntly, and to her amazement Lady Raytham shook her head.

"No, I've missed nothing; I shouldn't imagine he would steal. He may have, of course, but I shall be able to tell you more about that to-morrow. He was grossly insulting and left me at a second's notice."

"Have you been out?"

"Yes, I went to a dinner with Princess Anita Bellini; we intended going on to the theatre, but I had a headache and decided to return."

"What time did you come back?" asked Leslie.

Lady Raytham raised her eyes to the ceiling.

"It may have been half-past nine—probably a little earlier," she said. "We dined at a little restaurant which the princess knows—"

"And then you came back and had another dinner!" said Leslie steadily. "The table is still on the landing—set for two, so far as I could see."

For a second the woman was staggered out of self-control. Her hand went up to her lips.

"Oh, that?" she said awkwardly. "My friend Mrs. Gurden came later, and—and we gave her some supper."

Leslie shook her head.

"I wish you would be frank with me, Lady Raytham," she said. "The truth is, you didn't go out to dinner at all, did you?"

For a second the woman made no reply.

"I don't know what I did," she said.

Between despair and suppressed anger her voice was a wail.

"He drove everything out of my mind. Oh, if I had known! If I had known!"

She covered her eyes with her hands, and Leslie heard the sobs she could not stifle.

"What did he say to you before he went?" she asked inexorably.

Lady Raytham shook her head.

"I can't tell you. He was dreadful, dreadful!"

Leslie had waited this opportunity to fire her shot.

"He is in our hands," she said. "Shall we bring him here?"

The woman uncovered her eyes and stepped back with a little scream.

"Here? Here?" she said huskily. "My heavens, not here! He must go to the mort—"

She stopped herself, but too late.

"How did you know he was dead?" asked Leslie sternly.

Under the rouge the woman's face was gray.

CHAPTER VII.
LESLIE'S INTERVIEW

"How did you know he was dead?" asked Leslie again. "Who told you?"

"I—I heard." Her voice was hardly more than a whisper.

"Who told you? Nobody knows but the inspector and me, and I have come straight away from the place where he was found. I left him three minutes ago."

"Three minutes? I don't understand." And then, as she saw that she had been trapped for the second time, the colour came and went in Jane Raytham's face.

"I don't wonder that you are surprised, Lady Raytham! You know that Barnes Common is a little more than three minutes away, don't you?"

The woman looked round like some hunted animal seeking an avenue of escape.

"I know he is dead," she said desperately.

And then she faced the girl with a new resolution and a courage which Leslie could only admire.

"I know he's dead!" she exclaimed. "I know he's dead! Heaven knows who killed him, but I found him there. I saw him as my car was passing—on the sidewalk. I somehow knew it was he and got out. That is how I know. I should have told the police, I suppose, but I was frightened, terribly frightened. I thought I should faint."

"Where were you going when you found his body?"

Leslie's grave eyes were fixed on the woman.

"To—to the Princess Bellini. She has a house in Wimbledon."

"But you couldn't have parted with her for very long, when you decided to follow her."

Jane Raytham licked her dry lips.

"She left something behind—the night was rather pleasant—I wanted the air, so I drove—"

"Won't you sit down, Lady Raytham?" said the girl gently.

The woman looked ready to drop. With a little nod she sank down into an easy-chair that was near at hand.

Humanity was at the back of Leslie Maughan's suggestion, but there was something else. She had learned at Scotland Yard never to interrogate either a prisoner or a possible witness while you are on the same level with them. It was a piece of information that had been conveyed to her by the greatest of the criminal counsel of the Bar. "Put a witness on a lower level," he said, "and he'll tell you the truth."

Now she looked down at the broken woman who was nervously fingering the arm of the chair, and a wave of pity swept over Leslie Maughan, such as she had never experienced before.

"You were not going to Princess Bellini's, Lady Raytham," she said gently. "You were looking for Druze; he had taken something of yours."

Lady Raytham gazed at her without answering.

"You thought he had gone to the Princess Bellini's. Is that the way, across Barnes Common?"

"It is—a way—yes."

"Then you saw the body and recognized it? Saw it in the light of your headlamps, as we did? You weren't on your way to Wimbledon at all; you were coming back. I saw the rear lights of your car!"

Lady Raytham was breathing quickly.

"How do you know?" she asked.

"You wouldn't have seen the body otherwise. It lay on the left-hand foot-path as you came toward London, on the farther path as you came from London. What kind of a car have you?"

Jane told her.

"So you had been to Princess Bellini? And what did Princess Bellini tell you?"

"She was not at home."

Instinctively Leslie Maughan recognized that Jane Raytham was speaking the truth now.

"So you came back, and you found the body? Searched it?"

The woman nodded.

"What were you seeking?"

Again the quick movement of tongue across parched lips.

"I can't tell you."

Suddenly Leslie looked round. Noiselessly crossing the floor, she turned the handle quickly and jerked open the door. Mrs. Gurden nearly fell into the room.

"Are you fearfully interested?" asked Leslie. Her tone was almost sweet.

The discomfited eavesdropper grimaced and tittered hysterically.

"I was just coming in—really, it was very awkward. My shoe lace came unfastened and I was just stooping. I don't know whatever you think of me, but you really must believe me, Miss Maughan, you really must! I think prying and spying people are simply dreadful, don't you, dear?"

"I do, dear!" said Leslie dryly, and pointed to the stairs. "Would you mind sitting on the bottom step until I come down?"

Greta went tittering down the stairs.

"Was she listening? Was she?" Lady Raytham asked the question with unusual energy.

"No, I don't think she had been there long. I have an uncanny knowledge when I am being overheard. I had it just at that moment. Lady Raytham, where is your emerald necklace?"

If she had struck the woman she could not have produced a more startling effect. Jane Raytham sprang to her feet with a low cry and put out a hand as though she were warding off some terrible menace. For a second her beautiful face was distorted with fear.

"Oh!" she gasped out. "Why do you say that?"

"Where is your necklace? Can I see it?"

Jane Raytham thought for a moment, her chin on her breast, and then slowly raised her eyes.

"Yes. Will you come with me?" she said in a whisper. Leslie followed her out of the room into the bedroom on the right that opened from the landing.

She switched on the lights, and they crossed to a corner of the room where on the wall hung, apparently, a small Rembrandt in a gilt frame. The picture must have been a very good copy, but it was no more. When Jane Raytham touched the frame it swung open like a door and showed behind a small, square safe set in the wall. Lady Raytham turned the key with a hand that shook—not even her iron nerve could conceal her emotion. Taking out a jewel box, she carried it to a table, pressed a hidden spring, and the lid flew open. And there the dumfounded Leslie saw the emerald chain—intact! Intact even to the square emerald pendant!

Leslie picked up the jewel and surveyed it in bewilderment. Then, opening her bag, she brought to light the emerald that had been found in the dead hand of Druze and placed it by the side of the pendant of the chain.

They were exactly alike.

"Are there two chains?" she asked.

"No," said Jane Raytham.

"Is that the one you wore to-night?"

She nodded.

Her eyes were flaming. Even under that terrible strain, she could not restrain her natural curiosity.

"Where did you get that?" she asked.

"We found it in Druze's hand," replied Leslie.

The woman's mouth opened in astonishment.

"You found—nothing else? No other—" Again she stopped quickly.

"No other part of the chain—no. Wasn't it this you were looking for?"

Leslie saw her expression change. Was it relief she detected? Certainly her tone was lighter and less strained when she spoke.

"No, I wasn't looking for that. Who killed him?"

"Who do you think?"

Eye to eye they stood, silent for the space of a second.

"Why should I suspect anybody?"

Leslie Maughan fired her second shot.

"Shall I suggest a name?" she asked. "Peter Dawlish!"

Again that quick upward jerk of the chin, as though she were meeting some sickening pain.

"Peter Dawlish?" she said loudly. "Peter Dawlish! You're mad—mad to think Peter Dawlish—"

Without warning, she stumbled forward and Leslie had only time to throw out her arms and take the weight of her as she fell in a swoon to the ground.

In a second Leslie had pressed the bell and had thrown open the door. The footman came running up.

"Open one of those windows, and get me some brandy."

He gaped down at the white-faced woman on the floor.

"Is her ladyship ill?" he asked.

"Don't ask questions! Open the window! Hurry."

And as the French windows were thrown violently open, she said:

"Now get the brandy."

Before the man had come back, Jane Raytham had opened her eyes and stared inquiringly up into the face that was bent to hers.

"What happened? I fainted. I'm a fool! Let us go out."

With Leslie's assistance she rose unsteadily to her feet.

"I'd better put your jewel case back in the safe, hadn't I? Or perhaps you'd rather do it?"

"It doesn't matter," said the woman listlessly.

And in that moment Leslie Maughan guessed why Anthony Druze had died.

Slipping her arm round Jane Raytham's waist, she took her back to the drawing room, insisted upon her lying on the couch, propping a pillow under her head, and throwing a heavy silken scarf that drooped on a chair back over her feet.

"You're very good," murmured Lady Raytham, "and I loathe you so much!"

"I suppose you do," said Leslie, "And yet you shouldn't, because I haven't been at all unpleasant."

Jane nodded her head in agreement.

"Will you keep very quiet when I tell you this? I haven't suggested that you will be under suspicion of shooting Druze."

She had no need to be a reader of faces to realize that this possibility had never occurred to Jane Raytham.

"I?" she said incredulously. "But how absurd! Why should I shoot? Oh, but that is impossible! It is impossible that anybody should think such a thing!" And, in spite of Leslie's warning, she struggled erect. "You don't think so, do you?"

She was on her feet, peering into the girl's face, her hand gripping Leslie's wrist fiercely.

"You don't think so? I hated Druze! I hated him, hated him!" She stamped her foot in her fury. "You don't know what it has meant to me—every morning to see his face, every minute liable to his presence. Do you realize what that meant? I had to school myself so that I didn't shudder at the sight of him, and the mock humility of his 'yes, my lady' and 'no, my lady' that I might sit unmoved at my own table and face my own husband, and appear oblivious to the horrible masquerade—"

She stopped, exhausted by her own vehemence.

Leslie waited a moment and then:

"What is Anthony Druze to you?"

Lady Raytham stared at her.

"To me—you mean— What do you mean?"

Suddenly she burst into a paroxysm of laughter. It was dreadful to see her.

"Oh, you fool! You little fool! Can't you guess? Don't you know?"

And then suddenly she ran out of the room. Leslie heard her bedroom door slam and the snap of the turning key and knew that her interview was ended.

CHAPTER VIII.
A SURPRISE FOR LESLIE

It was two o'clock when a taxicab stopped in Severall Street, Lambeth, and a very weary girl alighted. The detective whom she had asked by telephone to meet her was waiting at the corner of the street and ran toward her.

"You want Mrs. Inglethorne's, don't you, miss? The house is on the opposite side of the road."

He hurried across the street and knocked at a door. Twice and three times he knocked before a sash went up and the voice of Peter Dawlish asked:

"Who is it?"

He had hardly asked the question before he recognized the girl.

"I'll be down in a second!"

But before he could descend, the landlady herself made an appearance. She was a little tremulous of voice, more than a little whining, when she recognized the familiar countenance of the detective.

"Whatcher want? There's nobody here except my young man lodger and he's straight. A policeman recommended him."

"This lady is from Scotland Yard and she wishes to see him, Mrs. Inglethorne," said the detective soothingly. "Don't get worried."

"Worried! Me workin' my fingers to the bone and my old man in 'stir' though as innocent as a babe unborn—"

By this time Peter Dawlish had descended.

"Do you wish to see me?"

She nodded.

"Where can I see you? Can you come out and sit in the cab for a few minutes?"

"Certainly."

"There is another favour I want to ask you. Will you be very annoyed if I ask you to allow this police officer to search your room?"

He was struck dumb for a second.

"Certainly! Why, is something lost?"

"Nothing." She turned to the detective and gave him instructions in a low tone; he pushed past the frightened landlady and went upstairs.

"Now come into the cab. You won't catch cold?"

He laughed irritatedly.

"I'm so hot with righteous indignation that I would melt an iceberg!" he said.

He stepped into the taxi and pulled the door tight.

"Now, Miss Maughan!"

She looked sideways at him; the white face of the lantern illuminating the taximeter formed a reflector that gave some light to the interior of the car.

"What have you been doing all evening?" she asked.

"From what hour?"

"Eight o'clock."

"I've been in the house. A job came to me this morning addressing envelopes and I've been working since seven till within a few minutes of your arrival. About two thousand of them are already addressed; I think that accounts for my time. I only had the envelopes and lists at six-thirty. Why, what has happened?"

"Druze is dead."

"Dead?"

"Murdered! His body was found on Barnes Common some time between eleven forty-five and midnight."

He whistled softly.

"That is a bad business. How was he killed?"

"Shot—at close range."

He was silent for a time.

"Naturally, after my wild and woolly threats, you suspected me. Come up and see the envelopes. My bedroom is the only decent room in the house."

She hesitated, then, stretching out her hand, pulled back the lock of the door.

Mrs. Inglethorne was past surprising. She stood at the foot of the stairs, an old ulster over her dressing gown, and watched the two go up without comment.

"There is nothing here, miss," said the detective before he caught sight of Peter. "Nothing except these." He indicated with a wave of his hand a deal table covered with small envelopes neatly packed.

Leslie smiled.

"You needn't have told me you'd been working here, Mr. Dawlish," she said. "It is like a smoke room!"

The aroma of cigarettes still hung about in spite of the open windows; the tin she had sent to him was on the table, only half full.

"I've been a little extravagant," he said apologetically, "but the temptation was great."

The detective still lingered by the door, evidently in two minds as to whether it would be proper to leave them in this peculiar environment. Leslie saved him the responsibility of a decision by:

"Thank you very much. I will be down in a minute or two," she said.

She sat at the foot of the bed, her arm over the rail, and looked at Peter. She would not have recognized him; he was clean-shaven, spruce. There was a certain buoyancy in his attitude which was new to her. Good-looking, too, and in spite of his approaching thirty years and all that he had suffered, remarkably youthful. It added a piquant interest to her scrutiny that she knew so much about his past—so much more than he guessed.

A husky voice hailed them from the foot of the stairs.

"Would you like a cup of tea, miss?"

Peter Dawlish looked at the girl with a smile.

"She really makes rather good tea," he said in a low voice.

"I should love one," she nodded, and he called softly down the stairs and came back.

"I'm scared of waking Elizabeth," he said, and added: "You look fagged!"

"Which means that I look hideous," she retorted with a frank smile. "I won't bandy compliments with you, or I would congratulate you upon the marked improvement which the barber has brought about. Did you know Druze very well?"

"Not very well," he said.

"Tell me something about him—all that you know."

He frowned at this, evidently trying to remember matters that had passed, facts that had gone out of his recollection.

"He came to Lord Everreed's place soon after I took up my post," he said. "My aunt the Princess Bellini recommended him—"

"The princess recommended him?" she said quickly. "Why? Was he in her service?"

"Yes," he nodded. "He was with Aunt Anita in Java for years. Her husband held some sort of minor post on one of the plantations: he was, I believe, a fairly poor man. After his death she came to England, and Druze came with her; in Java she had afforded the luxury of a butler; living is rather cheap there, but when she came to England she got rid of him. I have a distinct recollection of the letter she wrote to Lord Everreed, which I answered. I call her 'aunt,' " he explained, "although she was only the half sister of my father, and in reality no relation to me at all. How long Druze remained with Lord Everreed, of course I do not know. From the date of my conviction that page of history is closed. But a few years after I had gone to prison I heard in a roundabout fashion—I think it was in a letter which an old servant of ours wrote—that he had gone into the service of Lady Raytham."

She thought over this for some time.

"When were you arrested?"

"Seven and a half years ago."

She looked up in surprise.

"Then you served the full sentence?"

He nodded.

"Yes. I am not on ticket-of-leave. The truth is, I was rather a troublesome prisoner. I suppose most prisoners are who have the delusion of innocence. Why do you ask?"

"I have reason to believe that the princess thought you only served five," said the girl. "But that really doesn't matter. I suppose she's of an age that— I'm being cattish! Now, tell me something more."

"You look a very sleepy cat," he said, and at that moment there came through the door a strange little figure.

How old she was it was difficult to tell, but Leslie guessed her to be six, though she was tall for that age. She was painfully thin, and her little arms, which carried with solemn attention a cup of tea, were hardly more than of the thickness of the bones that showed through the flesh. Her face, pinched and thin and translucent, had a beauty which made the girl catch her breath. She raised two big eyes to survey the visitor, and then the long lashes fell on her cheeks.

"Your tea," she said.

Leslie took the cup gently from the child's hand and set it down.

"What's your name?" she asked, and as she put her hand on the yellow head, the little creature shrank back, her face puckered with fear.

"That's Belinda!" said Peter, with a smile.

The child wore a ragged old mackintosh over a nightgown that had once been of red flannelette, but which had washed to the palest of pinks. Her hands, lightly clasped before her, were almost transparent.

"I'm Mrs. Inglethorne's little girl," she said in a low voice. "My name is 'Lizabeth—not Belinda."

She raised her eyes quickly to the man and dropped them again. The gravity of her tone, the low sweetness of her voice, amazed Leslie Maughan. For a second she forgot that she was too tired to be interested even in the bizarre.

"Won't you come and talk to me?"

The child glanced at the door.

"Mother wants me."

"Talk to the lady!"

Evidently Mrs. Inglethorne at the bottom of the stairs had good ears. The child started, looked apprehensively round and came sidling toward Leslie.

"What do you do with yourself?" asked Leslie. "Do you go to school?"

Elizabeth nodded.

"I think about Daddy most of the time."

Leslie remembered that Daddy was at that moment serving his country in Dartmoor.

"I keep him in a book; he's very nice—ever so nice." The child nodded soberly.

"In a book?" asked Leslie. "What kind of a book?"

A voice outside the door supplied an answer. Mrs. Inglethorne must have crept up the stairs to listen better.

"Don't take no notice of her, miss; she's a bit cracked! Any good-looking feller she sees in a book she says is her father! Why, she used to take the king once, and then Lord what's-his name; and when I think of her own poor dear father that worked his fingers to the bone and got a 'stretch' for nothing, as innocent as a babe unborn—it's very hard—"

Elizabeth was tense now; her big eyes narrowed, her ear turned to the door. It was an attitude of apprehension, and Leslie's heart ached for the child. She smoothed her hair, and this time the little girl did not shrink.

"I'll send you some wonderful pictures and you'll be able to make up fathers and uncles and all sorts of nice things from them."

Stooping, she kissed the child, and with her arm about her painfully thin shoulders led her to the door. On the landing the unhealthy-looking Mrs. Inglethorne smirked and squirmed, a picture of gratitude for the lady's condescension.

"I'm going to be very interested in Elizabeth," said Leslie, her steady eyes on the woman. "You won't mind if I come round sometimes to see how she is getting on?"

Mrs. Inglethorne made a fearful grimace which was intended to express her pleasure.

"How many children have you?"

"Five, miss."

The woman was looking at her curiously, possibly fascinated by her first meeting with the female of the hated species.

"Five in this little house?" Leslie raised her eyebrows. "Where do you keep them all?"

Again the woman wriggled, this time uncomfortably.

"In the kitchen, miss, except the two girls; they sleep in my room."

"I'd like to have a look at your kitchen."

"It's a bit late and you'd wake 'em up," said Mrs. Inglethorne after hesitation.

But Leslie waited, and reluctantly Mrs. Inglethorne went down the stairs, the girl following. The kitchen was at the back of the house, approached by a narrow passage. It was a room barely ten feet square, cold and miserably furnished. In the unsatisfactory light of the oil lamp the woman carried she saw not three but four little bundles; one, a child which could not have been three years old, slept in a soap box on the floor. Its coverlet was a strip of dusty carpet which had been roughly cut to fit the shape of the box. Two children were huddled together under the table, wrapped in an old army overcoat. The fourth lay in a corner under a flour sack, so still that she might have been dead: a girl of eleven, sandy-haired, sharp-featured, who shivered and groaned in her sleep as the light of the lamp came upon her face.

"It's very 'ard on a woman who's got five mouths to fill," complained Mrs. Inglethorne, "but I wouldn't part with 'em for the world! And it's warm in the kitchen when we've had a coke fire going all evening."

Leslie went out of that sad little room sick at heart. Poverty she had seen and understood. Possibly these unfortunate children were as well off as thousands of others in the great metropolis. The weaklings would die; the fittest would survive and drag their stunted bodies to a free school where they would be taught just enough to enable them to write their betting slips and read the football reports intelligently.

Peter was waiting for her at the foot of the stairs.

"I think I'll go home now. I'm rather tired," she said. "Most likely you will be interrogated to-morrow either by Mr. Coldwell or an officer from the Yard. I think the best thing you can do is to go up and interview him."

And then, abruptly:

"Have you seen your mother since you have been free?"

He shook his head.

"My parent has expressed her wishes on the matter in unmistakable terms. We were never *en rapport*, so to speak, and perhaps it is a little too late now to attempt to arrive at a mutual understanding."

She looked down at the floor, her lips pursed.

"I wonder," she said, and held out her hand. "Good-night, Peter Dawlish."

He took the hand, held it for a second, and then:

"You're rather wonderful. I'm getting a new angle on life," he said.

She had one more call to make. Inspector Coldwell had promised to wait at Scotland Yard until she returned with her report, and she found him sipping coffee in the lobby, and told him briefly the result of her visit.

"I never thought Peter knew much about it. What does he know of Druze?"

He listened intently until she had finished.

"Rum! All the paths in this maze lead back to the Princess Bellini. Yes, I'll see Peter; I'll wire him in the morning," he said, yawning. "It is time all honest people were in bed. I'm going to take you home."

Her cab was waiting, and though she had no need of an escort, he pointed out that her way was largely his.

"What we're going to do about Lady Raytham I don't know. I'm taking it for granted that you have discovered a whole lot that you haven't told me."

"Not a whole lot, a little," she admitted.

Mr. Coldwell scratched his head.

"That little is usually crucial. However, I am not going to discourage you. Keep your mystery; a little romance in police work has a wonderful tonic value."

The cab carried them across deserted Trafalgar Square, and a few seconds later stopped before the door of Leslie's flat.

"I suppose you know all that is to be known about the case?" he said, with a touch of the sardonic, as he handed her out of the cab. "Whilst I, a poor old muddle-headed copper, am groping round like a blindfolded man in a fog!"

"I think I know a lot," she admitted, with a tired smile.

Coldwell was amused.

"The complacency of the woman! Here she is, keeping all her clues up her sleeve, ready to spring them out and reduce police headquarters to a bewildered pulp! Know all about Druze, do you?"

"I know a lot about him."

"Fine!" said Coldwell.

She had the door open now, and he waited until she was in the passage before he dropped his bombshell.

"Promise me you won't come out and ask questions, but will go straight up to bed, if I tell you something?"

"I promise," she said.

He put his hand on the knob of the door, ready to shut it.

"Arthur or Anthony Druze, as he was variously called, was a woman!"

The door slammed on her; before she recovered from her stupor she heard the rattle of the cab as it moved away.

CHAPTER IX.
DRUZE'S HANDICAP

Druze—a woman! It was incredible—almost impossible! Yet that shrewd old man would not have jested with her. She dragged herself up the stairs, her limp body aching for rest, her mind very wide awake and alert.

Druze a woman! She shook her head helplessly. And then she remembered Lady Raytham's hysterical laughter. "What was Druze to you?" Jane Raytham knew!

Leslie was too sane, too big, to feel foolish. She stopped on the landing and leaning heavily on the balustrade, she recalled the hairless face and figure of the portly butler. All her theories must go by the board. A scaffolding must be erected on a new foundation.

She found Lucretia Brown huddled up in a chair before a dead fire, fast asleep. Lucretia had never been trained out of her habit of "waiting up." It was her firm conviction that only this practice of hers saved her mistress from a terrible fate. She woke with a start and came reeling to her feet.

"Oh, miss!" she gasped out. "What time is it?"

Leslie glanced at the mantelpiece.

"Three o'clock," she said, "and a fine morning! Why aren't you in bed, you poor, knock-kneed girl?"

"I'm not knock-kneed and never was," protested Lucretia. "Three o'clock, miss? What a time!" She shivered. And then, morbidly curious: "Has anything been up, miss?"

"More things are 'up' than will ever come down, I think," replied Leslie, as she dropped into a chair. "There's been a murder."

"Good heavens!" said the shocked Lucretia. And then, with pardonable curiosity: "Who done it?"

"If I knew 'who done it,' I'd be a very contented female."

Leslie stifled a yawn.

"Run the bath, Lucretia, make me some hot milk, and don't wake me till ten o'clock."

"If I'm awake then," said Lucretia ominously. "I never see such a place as this. You turn night into day. Did he have his throat cut?" She returned to the tragedy.

"No. I'm sorry to disappoint you, but it was quite ghastly enough."

She dragged herself to her feet and went to her desk, turning over the letters that had arrived by the night mail. There was one which looked promising. She tore off the end of the envelope, read its contents, and locked the document away in a drawer. A little while later, before Lucretia had run the water from the bath, Leslie Maughan, snug between sheets, was sleeping dreamlessly.

She woke with a dim remembrance of the rattle of teacups and of Lucretia's calling her. Partly opening her eyes, she saw the cup by her bedside. She was horribly tired; bed was a warm and luxurious place; she must have dozed for the sound of voices wakened her.

Her bedroom led from her sitting room and the door was half open. Two people were speaking—Lucretia and somebody else whose voice was familiar.

"I will wait. Please don't wake Miss Maughan especially for me."

Leslie sat up in bed. Through the closing door which the maid was jealously guarding, she saw the big, straight figure of a woman. Lady Raytham! In an instant she was out of bed, thrust her feet into slippers, and pulled her dressing gown about her. She stopped only at the mirror to brush back her hair.

Lady Raytham was standing in the middle of the study, a bright coal fire was burning, and the room, at that early hour of the morning, had a special attraction for its young owner. But Jane Raytham's presence seemed, for some unaccountable reason, to lend it a new distinction, as a great bunch of Easter lilies, or a bowl of narcissus, might have done.

"Good-morning. I'm sorry to be so early. I hope I did not disturb you?"

She was polite, almost frigidly so, and Leslie could only look at her in wonder. All the evidence of distress and terror that had marked her face on the night before had vanished—all except that dark tint under the eyes.

"Won't you sit down? Have you had breakfast?" asked Leslie practically.

Lady Raytham shook her head.

"Please don't bother about me. I have plenty of time and can wait," she said.

There was a certain resentful admiration in her gaze; she was thinking how few women of her acquaintance were presentable at such an hour and in such circumstances. She had never seen Leslie Maughan in the daytime before, and not only did she stand the test of the cruel morning light, but she looked even prettier. She liked the poise of the girl and the readiness with which she accepted this sensible suggestion and disappeared into the bathroom, the gawky maid, her arms laden with garments, following. By the time she came out, Lucretia Brown had laid a little table; huge blue coffee cups and china racks bristling with crisp brown toast.

"No, I couldn't eat, thank you." Lady Raytham shook her head. "I will have some coffee."

Leslie looked significantly at the door and Lucretia regretfully disappeared.

"Yes, I slept," said Jane Raytham listlessly. "I don't know how or why, but I did. I suppose I just couldn't sleep any more. There is nothing about the murder in the newspapers."

Leslie made a mental calculation.

"There wouldn't be; it will be in the evening press. I know all about Druze."

"You know—about her?" Jane Raytham looked at her steadily.

"What was her name?" asked Leslie, but the other woman shook her head.

"I don't know; she was always Druze to me."

"Did your husband know—"

"That she was a woman?" She shook her head. "No. Poor Raytham! He'd have had a fit! But then, he never notices anything."

She had married the first Baron Raytham when he was a little over fifty, bachelor-minded, a man of set habits, who had found himself most unexpectedly a benedict and was a little aghast at the discovery. For the greater part of a year he had striven to be the model husband, and had been something of a bore. The domestic habit was foreign to him. Society and all its dainty et ceteras he loathed. Before the end of the first year of their married life, he had given up all attempt to interest himself in the new complexities which marriage had brought. Thereafter he devoted his energies and thoughts to his concession—his boards of directors, balance sheets, and all the precious things which were life for him—and Jane Raytham was left very much to her own devices.

"My husband is very seldom in London—probably not two months a year. He has"—she hesitated—"other interests."

Very wisely, Leslie did not pursue the subject. She too had heard that Lord Raytham had carried into married life a loose string or two that was substantially attached and which he was unwilling or unable to drop. Leslie was too versed in the ways of the world to be shocked at this; too sophisticated to be anything but mildly amused at the inefficiency of man, who finds it so easy to get rid of a wife and so difficult to discharge a feminine attachment.

"Your name is Leslie, isn't it?" And, when she nodded: "I wonder if you would mind my 'Leslie-ing' you? You're not so formidable as I thought. I—I rather like you. My name is Jane—if you ever feel friendly enough to 'Jane' me—I've been abominably rude to you, but now I've come to ask you for favours."

Leslie laughed.

"I owe you an apology," she said, and the other woman was quick to see her meaning.

"About Druze? It would be a beastly idea, only—women are such queer fools, aren't they? No, I knew Druze was a woman; that made everything so hideous. I wonder if you will believe me when I say that that was almost my heaviest cross—almost."

"What was really the heaviest?" asked Leslie quietly.

Lady Raytham fetched a long sigh and looked out of the window.

"I don't know. It is rather difficult to compare these things." And then, quickly: "Of course, I know now which is the heaviest, but that is so new and so crushing that I dare not let myself think about it. Something Druze said to me before she went out; something she told me that froze my blood." She closed her eyes and shuddered, but recovered instantly. "That is why I got my car and went in search of her. She told me a little but not everything, and I had to know! My first thought was—you'll think I'm a hypocrite—that Peter had killed her. If I thought at all! I don't think I cared. I had only one idea in my mind, to find something she had boasted about."

"Not the necklace?"

Jane Raytham smiled contemptuously.

"The necklace! As if I cared for that! I'm making a clean breast of every-thing—up to a point. The necklace you saw at the house last night was only—"

"Was a copy, I know that," said Leslie quietly. "An exact replica of the real emerald chain, and, valueless! When you didn't bother to put it back in the safe, I guessed."

Eye met eye, each striving to read the other's thoughts.

"What else did you guess?" asked Jane Raytham, after a long silence, and then:

"No, no, don't tell me. I want to feel that nobody knows that—nobody! You will tell me that I am trying to create a fool's paradise myself, and I'm a moral coward. I wonder if I am." And then, obliquely: "Have you seen Peter?"

"I saw him last night, yes. He knew nothing about the murder—not so much as you," said Leslie.

The woman ignored this challenge.

"I wonder how much you do know, Leslie?"

It was a strain to ask the question. Even as she had her reservations, so also had Leslie Maughan. The truth must come from Jane Raytham or not be truth at all.

"I know you were being blackmailed; that the necklace you gave was part of the price; the twenty thousand pounds, which I imagine was all you could raise in cash, was the other part. I guess also that Druze was a blackmailer. Am I right?"

Jane nodded. There was a perceptible brightening of her face as though, fearing to hear worse, she was experiencing relief at the limitation of the girl's knowledge.

"How long have you been paying?"

She did not answer, and Leslie repeated the question.

"I don't know. Quite a long time."

Another silence. The truth was not to come yet, then, only a measure of it.

"Do you want to tell me any more?" she asked.

Jane Raytham drooped her head. She wanted to tell—just as much as this frank and friendly girl knew, hoping against hope that the more precious secret would remain with her, and yet almost praying that Leslie Maughan would suddenly drag forth the grisly skeleton and expose it to her eyes.

"Yes, I want to, terribly! But I shan't. I can't bring myself to put things into words. And I want your help. How badly I need it! But, my dear, you're police, part of the machinery of Scotland Yard. I've told you too much already. I shall be living in a flutter of fear all day—"

"I'm Leslie Maughan in this flat," said Leslie, smiling. "Just a sort of little sister of the human race! But I'll warn you that I am determined, as far as I can, to find the murderer of that wretched woman. Short of that information you can tell me anything."

Jane shook her head ruefully.

"I don't know who killed Druze. I will not swear that, but I will tell you on my word I don't know; I do not even suspect. Anita wanted to know. I called on her this morning. She is like a woman distraught. I never knew she felt so deeply. The police have been there to inquire whether Druze called. I suppose you told them last night that I had told you. Poor Anita! She was terribly fond of Druze, who was once in her service. She always contended that he hadn't been, and talked about him as though he were the merest stranger. But that, I think, was her pride; she hated the thought that she had ever been so poverty-stricken that she was obliged to let him go—her, I mean. The habit of years takes a lot of breaking! I have thought of Druze as a man and spoken of him as a man so long, that it is difficult to get out of the trick."

"One question I want to ask you, Lady—Jane, I'd better call you. It will be almost as difficult a habit to get into! Did Druze forge Lord Everreed's name as Peter Dawlish thinks he did?"

Jane Raytham shook her head.

"That is impossible," she said simply.

"Why impossible?"

The answer took Leslie Maughan's breath away.

"Because she could not read or write!"

CHAPTER X.
A DOCTOR'S CONFESSION

"Druze was illiterate, but, like all illiterate people, had acquired a certain form of culture and was very clever to conceal this misfortune. I think, in fact I know, she had the schooling of an average child, but she was just incapable of learning. The Council schools and even the public schools are full of people like that, of girls and boys familiar with the most obscure sciences who have never mastered these elementary arts."

Leslie thought quickly.

"Her signature was on the passport?"

"I wrote it," said the surprising woman. "She told me she wanted to go across to France for a week-end trip and asked me if I would sign the passport form. That was only a few weeks ago, so it is fresh in my mind. Now tell me what I am to do? The police will come to me, and I am prepared to tell them the truth, though I cannot see how I can help them."

"The whole truth?" asked Leslie significantly.

Jane Raytham looked at the girl for a long time before she answered.

"As much as I've told you—not as much as you guess," she said, in her even voice.

Leslie carried her cup of coffee to the desk.

"Would you like me to write down the gist of what you have said, and sign the statement?" she asked. "That might save you an awful lot of trouble."

Jane hesitated.

"Is it necessary? I suppose it is," she said. "Yes, if you would be so kind."

For ten minutes she watched the girl as her pen flew over the paper, and took the pages from her as they were written.

"You have put my case more cleverly than I could have put it myself," she said with a little smile. "I almost think you're sympathetic."

"You don't know how sympathetic I am," said Leslie, rising from her chair to make way for the other.

Lady Raytham sat down, read the last sheet again, and had dipped her pen in the ink, when the sound of voices came from outside the door. It was Lucretia's raised protest, and a deeper voice, which Leslie instantly recognized, and, running to the door, threw it open. The Princess Anita Bellini stood on the landing, glaring through her monocle at the defiant Lucretia.

"You can't come in—Miss Maughan's engaged," she was saying. "I don't care if you're a princess or if you're the Queen of Sheba. When Miss Maughan's engaged, nobody can—!"

"That will do, Lucretia. Come in, Princess."

The big woman strode into the apartment without a word of thanks, not even deigning to look at the defiant maid.

"Where is—" she began, and then she saw Lady Raytham at the desk. "What are you writing, Jane?" she demanded loudly. "You're not being such a fool as to make a statement to the police, are you?"

"Lady Raytham is merely telling me as much as I already know," said Leslie.

"Jane, you must not sign it. I forbid it!"

There was a tremor of anger in the hard voice, and, looking at the woman, Leslie saw how deeply the tragedy must have affected her. She seemed ten years older. The big slit of a mouth was turned down at the ends, the eyes red and inflamed.

Very calmly Lady Raytham affixed her signature.

"Don't be foolish, Anita," she said quietly. "The police are entitled to know certain things about Druze."

"What have you told them? Can I see this precious document?"

She reached out her hand, but Leslie was before her.

"Let me read it to you, Princess," she said, and placed the desk between herself and her furious visitor. That Princess Bellini was in a cold tremble of rage was patent.

She read without interruption to the end.

"Jane Raytham, you're a fool to sign a thing like that!" stormed the woman. "Let them find things out without committing yourself to paper. This girl has tricked you into a confession—"

"Confession?" said Leslie, with a smile. "How absurd! Lady Raytham knew that Druze was a woman; it was impossible that she should not. And, as she says, she has only told us what we already knew, and what you already knew."

"I knew nothing," said Anita Bellini harshly, her baleful eyes fixed on the girl, "except that you have tricked Lady Raytham into making a statement which will involve her in considerable trouble."

Leslie faced her squarely, and for the first time Anita Bellini became dimly and uncomfortably conscious of the strength of this inconsiderable person. They had met before, and the honours of that meeting had not rested with the princess. But she had thought of Leslie as a girl with a certain glibness of tongue, a gift of smart repartee, but without any of the especial qualities that she might expect in a foe worthy of her heaviest metal. But now it had dawned upon her that, whether she was "Coldwell's pretty typist," as she had contemptuously referred to her, or whether she was "a Scotland Yard underling," she was certainly a factor to be considered and forestalled. And if she had had any doubt on the subject, Leslie Maughan's first words would have dispelled it.

"Lady Raytham has made a statement, and you also will make a statement, Princess," she said, "either before or after the inquest."

The woman surveyed her with an oddly sly look that was unnatural in her.

"I don't know how you can bring me in," she began, and her tone was milder than it had been.

"You employed Druze. Apparently you knew she was a woman, and are acquainted with her early history," said Leslie quietly. "That is quite sufficient to bring you into any inquiry which the police set afoot."

Anita Bellini took out her monocle, polished it on her handkerchief and returned it to her eye.

"Possibly I was rather precipitate," she said. "But I think you should make allowance for my—whatever I have said. I have been awfully upset by Druze's death. Would you read the statement again?"

It was a very simple record of the information which Lady Raytham had given to the girl, and, when she had finished reading:

"No, there is nothing in that," said the princess. "I suppose this evidence has to come out. Does it mean that we shall be called at the inquest? I couldn't stand that, I couldn't!"

In that instant Leslie detected a tremor in the woman's voice. Anita Bellini, the formidable, had a weak spot, after all. But she recovered herself very quickly.

"If everybody had his due, Peter Dawlish would be under arrest," she said, and, ignoring the protests of Jane: "The man hated Druze; you know that quite well, Jane. He threatened her; I can prove it!"

And then, in a conciliatory tone:

"I hope we're not going to be bad friends, Miss Maughan. If I can help you I will. Is there any more you can tell me than appears in the evening newspaper?"

"Nothing," said Leslie shortly.

They left together soon after, but before they departed, Leslie found an opportunity of speaking a few words to Jane Raytham.

"I don't want you to tell anybody about the necklace," she said in a low voice, as she accompanied her down the stairs. "Especially about the emerald that was found in Druze's hand. You promise me? Or have you already told?"

Jane Raytham shook her head.

"I wondered why you hadn't put that in the statement," she suggested. "But you may trust me. I shall not speak about it, even to Anita."

At that moment the voice of the princess hailed her from the foot of the stairs and further conversation became impossible.

———————

Leslie arrived at Scotland Yard just before twelve, and was mounting the stone stairs as Peter Dawlish came down.

"A clean bill," he said with a smile. "At any rate, that is the impression Coldwell gives me. It seems that your detective man's search was a very thorough one; I suppose you know that he searched me also? And, by the way, Belinda sends her love."

"Belinda?" Leslie was momentarily bewildered. "Oh, you mean that little child, Elizabeth. How wicked! I had almost forgotten her!"

"She hasn't forgotten you," said Peter, and with a cheery wave of his hand went on.

She found Mr. Coldwell in his big, comfortable office, the stub of a cigar between his teeth, his bristling brows gathered in thought.

"Just going to phone you," he mumbled. "I've seen that man of yours, and I'm satisfied that he had nothing to do with the crime."

" 'That man of mine' being Peter Dawlish?" she said calmly. "You give me quite a proprietorial feeling!"

From her bag she took the statement that Lady Raytham had signed and laid it on the table before him. He read it through carefully, folded it up and slipped it into a drawer.

"Did you tell Anita Bellini about the emerald we found in Druze's hand?" he asked.

"No," she said. "That's the last thing in the world I should have told her; I asked Lady Raytham not to tell either. Why?"

He smiled grimly.

"Thought you hadn't," he said. "Her Serenity called me on the phone five minutes ago, and said she'd read in one of the newspapers that something very valuable had been found on Druze's person. I haven't seen all the newspapers, but those I've read make no mention of the emerald, and I don't see why they should, unless they are psychic. The princess suggested, rather than said, that you had confirmed this mythical newspaper report."

Leslie shook her head in admiration.

"That woman is certainly a quick worker," she said. "What did you tell her?"

Mr. Coldwell relit his cigar with the exasperating deliberation of his age.

"I told her that we *had* found something valuable—a packet of money. She seemed kind of disappointed."

The telephone bell shrilled; he picked up the receiver, listened in silence for a time, and then:

"All right, I'll come down," he said.

"The Lambeth police have got a quaint clue—a kind of ready-made one, but it should be investigated, as it has to do with your Peter. Would you like to come along?"

She looked at him steadily.

"If you refer to him as my Peter again, I shall be very offensive to you, Mr. Coldwell," she said, and Coldwell scratched his chin.

"Somehow he seems to belong to you; I don't know why I get that impression."

Her eyes wandered to a corner of the room and for the first time she saw the two big travelling trunks. They were new and bore the label of the Cunard Steamship Company.

"Druze's," he said laconically. "We'll go through those when we come back."

It was at the corner of Severall Street that the taxicab stopped. The local subdivisional inspector was waiting, and with him a detective.

"Let me have a look at that paper," said Coldwell immediately, and Leslie, who had not heard the one-sided conversation on the telephone, wondered what was coming next.

The inspector took a dirty slip of paper from his pocketbook and placed it in Coldwell's hand. He fixed his glasses and read, then passed the slip to the girl. The message was written in pencil and in an illiterate hand:

Dawlish keeps his gun under a loose board in his bedroom just as you go inside the door.

"Where did this come from?" asked Coldwell.

"It was delivered at the station just before I telephoned to you. A street lad brought it along. He said it had been handed to him by a man, who gave him a few coppers for his trouble. I thought it best that you should know."

They walked down the street toward Mrs. Inglethorne's house and the door was opened immediately by that lady, who was surprisingly clean and spruce. She seemed surprised, but was certainly not agitated by the appearance of the police officers.

"Yes, sir, Mr. Dawlish has just come in. Shall I call him down?"

"No, thank you; we'll go up."

Coldwell mounted the stairs and knocked at the door of the front room, and a voice bade him come in. Over the inspector's shoulder, Leslie saw that Peter was sitting at a deal table, pen in hand, a stack of addressed envelopes before him. He shifted his chair round and his eyebrows rose in astonishment.

"Hello!" he said, obviously taken aback by the character of the call. "Do you want to see me again, Inspector?"

Coldwell took in the room at a glance.

"I have information that you've a gun concealed under this floor," he said. "If you don't mind I'll make another search."

"Fire ahead," said Peter, without a moment's hesitation.

Coldwell turned back to the door, lifted a corner of the faded carpet and saw the loose board immediately. To lift it up was the work of a second. Thrusting in his hand, he pulled out a long black Browning pistol. Peter's face went white; his jaw dropped in an amazement that could not have been simulated.

"Anything more here?" asked Coldwell, and, kneeling, thrust in his hand and groped about. Presently he found a small package wrapped in cloth and brought it to the light. He unwrapped it slowly.

"My stars!" gasped out a hollow voice.

Mrs. Inglethorne had crept up the stairs and was an interested spectator. There was reason enough for her astonishment, for in the centre of that dirty rag lay three large diamond rings, the least valuable of which must have been worth a hundred pounds.

"Do you know anything about these, Dawlish?"

Peter shook his head.

"No, I'm not a burglar," he said, with a return of his old good spirits. "That branch of the profession is not my forte, and that little find has every appearance of being the proceeds of a very old burglary."

Coldwell looked at the wrapper; it was thick with dust. Even as he turned back one corner of the rag, a fine cloud arose.

"Do you know anything about these, Mrs. Inglethorne?"

She shook her head.

"Or the pistol?"

The woman was paralyzed; her face had gone a ghastly gray as she realized the enormous significance of that find. There they had lain month after month, at least five hundred pounds' worth of jewellery, the results of one of her lodger's little coups, and she none the wiser.

"Never—seen—it!" Mrs. Inglethorne found a difficulty in breathing.

"This has been used as a hiding place before," said the inspector, as he laid the pistol and rings upon the deal table.

He examined the Browning, noted its make and number, and, having carefully removed the magazine and dislodged the cartridges from the chamber, smelled at the barrel.

"It has been fired recently, I should imagine: it still smells of cordite. Is this yours, Dawlish?"

"No, sir: I've never seen it before."

"Humph!" The inspector sat down on the bed in exactly the place where the girl had sat the night before. He looked round for Mrs. Inglethorne, but that woman had vanished.

"Nobody told you about that hiding place?"

"No, sir."

"Hello, Elizabeth!" It was Leslie's interruption. The frail child stood in the doorway, shyly smiling at the beautiful lady of her dreams.

She whispered something that the girl could not catch, and Leslie went nearer to her, took the two thin hands in hers, and, stooping, kissed the pale cheeks.

"Tea?" she said with a laugh. "No, dear, I don't think we want tea. It was very nice of you to come."

The child's eyes were fixed on the table; they were wide open, and in their depths Leslie saw a look of fear.

"What is it?" asked Leslie.

"That big gun," whispered the child. "Mother had it this morning, and I was so frightened."

The sharp-eared Coldwell heard.

"Your mother had it this morning, my dear?" he said kindly. "Where did she have it?"

"In the kitchen. A gentleman left it—a little gentleman with a yellow face. Mother brought it into the kitchen and said we all ought to be killed."

She clapped her hands to her mouth with an exclamation of fright, for only then did she remember the strict injunctions laid upon her. Coldwell strode out of the room to the head of the stairs and called Mrs. Inglethorne in a stentorian voice. It was a long time before he had an answer, and then by the tremulous voice he guessed that part of the conversation between himself and the child had been overheard.

"Come up here," he said curtly, and Mrs. Inglethorne came lumbering up the stairs.

"This pistol came to your house this morning. From whom?"

The woman's mouth was dry with terror. She blinked from one to the other.

"A gentleman brought it," she gasped out. "He said it belonged to Mr. Dawlish, and would I put it under the floor—without a word of a lie, sir—if I never move from here."

Coldwell's gimlet eyes searched her unwholesome face.

"You told me you had never seen the pistol before. Who sent it?"

She shook her head.

"I don't know, sir. I've never seen the man before in my life—if I never move—"

"You'll move!" said Coldwell grimly. "And darned quick, if you don't tell me the truth!"

But to her story she stuck, swearing by numerous gods, some of whom were unfamiliar to Leslie, that she knew nothing whatever of the pistol except that it had been brought there by a perfect stranger who she thought was a friend of Peter Dawlish.

To Leslie Maughan's astonishment the inspector appeared to accept this story, and to find nothing venal in the act of concealment.

"You did a very foolish thing, Mrs. Inglethorne. The next time a perfect stranger comes and asks you to conceal firearms in your lodger's room, you had better notify the police."

He slipped the pistol into his pocket, and looked round for Elizabeth, but she had vanished.

"That lets you out, Dawlish," he said. "At least, it does for the moment. If I were you, I would make an inspection of the room and see if there are other likely hiding places where stuff could be planted."

He had a consultation with the local inspector, and then he and Leslie walked back to their cab.

"You've let her down rather lightly, haven't you, Mr. Coldwell?"

He gave her a quick sidelong glance.

"Minnow fishing never did appeal to me," he drawled, "especially while one of the big pikes is hovering around, and it's the pike I'm after. And if this minnow doesn't lead me to him, I'll be astonished."

"You accept Peter Dawlish's story?"

He nodded, as he helped her into the cab. When he had followed and had slammed the rackety door and the machine was in motion, he explained.

"The detective who searched the house last night found that loose board and the hole underneath. He might have missed the diamond rings, but he couldn't have missed the gun. Therefore I knew it had been planted since. Peter might have put it there, of course, but the odds were all against that theory. The true story was the one told by the child. The little yellow-faced gentleman was probably one of the three who attacked Dawlish."

For the first time she learned of that surprising outrage which had been committed in Severall Street the night Peter had visited her.

He admitted a little irritably that the case had gone outside his own experience.

"Here's a woman who has been masquerading as a man for the past fifteen years, found dead, with an emerald in her hand, worth, at a rough guess, a thousand pounds. She was shot at close quarters with the pistol I have in my pocket—"

She gasped.

"You don't mean that?"

He nodded.

"I do mean it. I'd like to bet a month's pay that I'm right. You think a murderer would be crazy to put the very weapon in the hands of the police, knowing that the pistol has a number and its purchase can be traced—unless it was bought in Belgium, which is extremely likely. You haven't seen Druze since she was found, have you? Well, I'm not advising you to; all the details about her can be passed on. There's a big black-powder burn at the base of her right thumb, that is to say on the back of her hand. First thing I noticed when I examined the body was that powder burn."

"How did that come there?" asked Leslie.

"She fired an automatic—five or six shots in rapid succession—and got the backfire. One shot wouldn't have burned her; it must have been at least five. Look!" He showed his own hand, and a raw red mark, faintly tinged with black. "I was firing an automatic this morning to see what would happen, and I've got exactly the same mark as she has. I'm only making a guess, Leslie, but my guess is that Miss or Mrs. Druze was killed in self-defense; that she started the gunplay and got the worst of it."

Leslie caught her breath.

"Then where is the other body?" she asked quickly.

He stared at her open-mouthed.

"Other body?"

"She killed somebody first," said Leslie quickly. "Killed or desperately wounded. Such a woman as Druze would not carry a pistol unless she knew how to use it. If she knew how to use it and fired first, then somebody was badly hurt."

The old man took off his hat and scratched his head.

"That's the natural conclusion to reach," he said, "and I didn't reach it! And why I didn't reach it I don't know! Just let me think this out, will ye?"

The silence was unbroken until they reached Scotland Yard.

"I'm still thinking it out," he said dismally as he stepped out of the cab behind her and paid the taxi man.

There was a bearded man in the hall, doctor written in every line of him. He was talking to the officer at the desk, and evidently Coldwell was being pointed out to him, for he walked to the door to meet the inspector as he entered.

"You're Mr. Coldwell? My name is Simmson. I am Doctor Simmson of Marylebone Road."

"Yes, Doctor?" said Coldwell, politely attentive.

"A friend of mine has suggested that I should go to Scotland Yard and report rather a curious circumstance," he said awkwardly. "I have never done such a thing before, and I'm a little at sea as to how I should begin. But I have a patient who is suffering from a gunshot wound, and I am not quite satisfied as to how she received her injury, which is a slight one."

Coldwell was all attention now.

"Through the calf; no artery has been injured. And really, I feel I'm being terribly disloyal to a patient—"

"What is her name?" asked Coldwell.

"Mrs. Greta Gurden," was the reply.

CHAPTER XI.
THE DOCUMENT

The apartment that Greta Gurden occupied was on the first floor of a house in Portman Crescent. Hers was one of those artistic little flats that reflected every taste but her own. She slept in a red lacquer bed, ornamented by golden devils, a bargain acquired many years before in the Caledonian Market, and renovated by her own hands. Life is rather a tragedy for the lonely woman; there was a shadowy husband very much in the background, but he had either run away from her or was in a lunatic asylum or something equally unsatisfactory. She was one of the thousands who were endeavouring to keep an expensive establishment on an insufficient income. By profession she was a journalist; edited a mildly scurrilous little paper called *Mayfair Gossip* which enjoyed a very limited circulation, and in truth took up very little of her time. It was certainly not in the paper's interest that she fostered the delusion that her life was one of hectic gayety. For she was to be seen occasionally at the most exclusive night clubs; more frequently at less exclusive establishments of the same order, her visitations being governed entirely by the wealth and taste of her escort. And numerically she had many friends. Her expansiveness and lack of reticence had been tersely and uncharitably condemned into the vulgar word "gush." Still, however it might sicken the more sophisticated, it was very pleasant to those who discovered from her for the first time how important or good looking or well dressed they were, what taste, discrimination, or tact they displayed upon every conceivable occasion, and how anxiously or impatiently Greta was looking forward to their next meeting.

There were young men who took her out to dinner or to supper or to dances. There were middle-aged men, fathers of families, whose hearts she fluttered with the promise of adventure never to be fulfilled, who escorted her to the less expensive places of popular amusement. There were, too, women who hovered everlastingly on that no-man's-land between Suburbia and Mayfair, who courted her society and influence, under the mistaken impression that she had the entrée to the most select circles.

Mayfair Gossip was entirely the property of Anita Bellini, and it was an unprofitable concern, a fact Anita never failed to emphasize, when Greta called on a Friday for her weekly stipend, her only regular source of income. The princess was good to Greta in other ways. She gave her an occasional dinner, a discarded dress or two, marched her off to afternoon concerts, and employed her as a sort of unpaid secretary. Occasionally, windfalls came the way of Greta Gurden—fifty pounds here and there for some little service which she had rendered. And she had always a use for the money. There were new curtains to buy, a fascinating Chinese cabinet, or something that looked like a fascinating Chinese cabinet, a carved ivory Madonna—a fair copy of a master's art. She had a passion for picking up entirely useless articles. Her dining room was cluttered up with imitation oak. Birmingham-made suits of chain armour, Benares brass from the same enterprising city, a gutted spinet that served only as a sideboard for the display of imitation Bristol ware. There was even a pair of antlers over the doorway, and Greta was not above suggesting to her awe-stricken visitors that the twelve-pointer had been shot by her when she was the guest of the Duke of Blank at his little hunting box in Inverness-shire.

She enjoyed the services of one who was charlady in the morning and maid in the afternoon, and only to this unemotional lady was the real Greta ever revealed.

Mrs. Gurden lay in bed with a bandaged leg. Torn between terror that memory brought and fear of blood-poisoning and its horrible consequences—among other duties she contributed the health notes to *Mayfair Gossip*—she was a difficult patient.

Greta could not afford to neglect her daily duty to herself. Her face was indistinguishable under a mud pack, designed to preserve the face from the ravages of age, and her hands were inclosed in complexion gloves. Two dark eyes glared oddly from the mask of gray, and she spoke with some difficulty, due to the dried earth that plastered her cheeks. Just now she had an additional reason for annoyance.

"Tell her I can't see her and I won't see her. Tell her to come back at twelve o'clock."

"She's from Scotland Yard, ma'am."

"I don't care; I won't see her."

The obedient charlady disappeared into the outer room. Greta heard the murmur of voices, and after a while the woman came back.

"She says she'll wait till you're ready. She wants to know how you hurt your leg."

Greta had no need to stifle her fury. A sudden panic descended upon her.

"Bring me some hot water."

It took some time to remove the renovating mud, a little longer time to substitute perfumed creams and powder. A brief glimpse through an open door had revealed to Leslie Maughan the cause of the delay. She waited patiently, having some sympathy with woman's losing fight against the ravages of time and care. When at length she was admitted, it was the old Greta who smiled ecstatically.

"My dear! How wonderfully good of you to come! So sweet of you! I was so hoping that I should have another opportunity of meeting you. The princess is rather difficult, isn't she? I did so want to have a little chat with you the last time we met. I admire your style awfully. Won't you sit down somewhere? Yes, I've had an awful accident. I was cleaning my husband's pistol and it went off, but fortunately no bones were broken."

"Where did this happen?"

It was on the tip of Greta's tongue to say "here," but she thought better of it.

"At a country house where I was staying for the week-end. People are so careless. Imagine leaving a pistol loaded! I nearly died of fright!"

"What country house was this?" asked Leslie.

Greta knit her brows.

"What was the name of the place? I don't know the people very well. Somewhere in Berkshire."

"Was your husband there, Mrs. Gurden?"

"Er—no—but he had been staying at the place; left his box behind. I was rummaging through it and found his pistol, and it looked so awfully rusty and dirty that I thought I would clean it."

"Who else was hurt besides you?" asked Leslie quietly.

Greta shot a swift, suspicious glance at the girl.

"Nobody, thank goodness!" she said.

Leslie waited a second, then:

"Was this before or after Druze was killed?"

Under the rouge Greta's face went suddenly gray and pinched. She sat bolt upright in bed and stared at the girl.

"Dead?" she said huskily. "Druze is dead? It's a lie!"

"Druze is dead! She was found last night on Barnes Common—shot!"

" 'She?' " The woman's forehead was puckered into lines. " 'She?' What are you talking about? I was speaking of Druze."

"So was I," said Leslie. "Druze was a woman; you know that."

The open mouth, the wide eyes, every visible expression of amazement revealed without question Greta Gurden's ignorance of the "butler's" sex.

"A woman! Good heavens!"

She sank back on the pillows, exhausted by her emotion, her eyes fixed on the ceiling. But for those wide-open pools of darkness, Leslie would have thought that the woman had fainted. Presently she spoke.

"I've nothing to tell you. I shot myself by accident. I know nothing about Druze—nothing. Why should I? The accident occurred when I was in the country. I won't talk to you! I won't!"

She almost screamed the words.

Leslie realized that it would be cruel to question her more closely; the woman was so distressed that she might have hesitated even if she had not feared the effects of a further cross-examination upon one who was in the surgeon's hands.

"I will come along and see you when you're a little better, Mrs. Gurden," she said.

Greta made no answer.

As Leslie's cab turned out of the street, it passed a big car swinging round to enter the unpretentious thoroughfare, and the girl had a glimpse of the princess. She wished now that on some pretext or other she had stayed, that she might see the meeting between these two.

Anita Bellini mounted the stairs and, entering the apartment without knocking, summarily dismissed the charwoman, and Mrs. Hobbs, not unused to such cavalier treatment, departed meekly.

"Has Maughan been here?" she demanded, as she strode into Greta's room.

Her eyes narrowed as she caught sight of the haggard face.

"I see she has," she said grimly. "What did she come about?"

Greta raised herself on her elbow and pushed up her pillow to support her; she was trembling so that after a second she rolled back on the pillow with a groan.

"She wanted to know how I was wounded," she said at last.

"What did you tell her?" asked the princess impatiently. "For Heaven's sake pull yourself together, my good woman! How did she know you were wounded, anyway? Did you send an announcement to the newspapers?"

"I don't know how she knew, but she did. I told her that it was an accident, that I was cleaning my husband's pistol and it went off. Anita, is it true?"

"Is what true?" asked the princess roughly.

"Is it true that Druze is dead?"

"Yes."

"And that she was a woman?"

"I thought you guessed," said the Princess Anita. "Of course she was a woman."

"My stars, how awful!"

Anita Bellini's cold glance transfixed the invalid.

"What is the matter with you?" she demanded harshly. "Druze was—"

She stopped short.

"How long are you going to be in bed?"

Greta shook her head.

"I don't know; the doctor says another week at least."

"Did you tell her anything more? Really, Greta, you're not to be trusted, though I never dreamed that nosy little devil would find out about your being shot. I suppose the doctor reported it."

She stared down at the woman speculatively.

"I suppose I'd better give you some money," she said, with no great enthusiasm. "You look awful, you know that? You're not wearing well, Greta. All the mud in the world will not take those wrinkles from under your eyes. Why, you're old."

The red in Greta Gurden's face was natural: it came and went. Fury blazed in the dark eyes, for now Anita Bellini had touched her upon the rawest place of Greta's self-esteem and put into words, at this incongruous moment, all that this poor little *poseuse* feared. But it was Anita Bellini's way, to go off at spiteful tangents, to sting and hurt those from whom she expected unswerving loyalty. It was characteristic of her that at this moment, when her mind and spirit were tensed to meet the very real dangers which threatened her, she could go out of her way to humiliate her creature.

"You aren't able to attend to *Gossip*, of course. You're having the letters sent here?" she asked, and, when the woman nodded silently: "The last batch were valueless; there was a little bit about the Debouson woman, but I knew all about that. She isn't worth a penny; in fact, there's a bankruptcy petition out against her husband. You had better write a spicy paragraph about her; that is all the information is worth."

She was walking about the room as she spoke, stopping now and again to look, with a contemptuous lift of her lips, at the tawdriness of the imitations with which the room was stocked.

"I'm going to Capri in the spring," she said. "The new villa has been bought; I suppose I'd better take you along with me."

She did not see the malignity that shot from the dark eyes.

"The paper will have to go. It is becoming more and more useless. If you had had a spark of genius in you, Greta, you would have made that into a property. You are sure you told that detective girl nothing?"

"Nothing," said Greta, regaining control of her voice.

"What is this?"

Anita had stopped before a big secretaire, pulled down the flap and was examining a number of letters neatly tied in bundles.

"Are those the papers of mine that I asked you to put in order?"

"Yes."

The princess detached one letter from a bundle, read it and tossed it back.

"Most of these things can be burned," she said. "You found nothing of importance?"

"No, nothing."

Something in Greta's tone made the other turn her head.

"What's the matter with you?"

And then the pent-up fury of Greta Gurden burst forth. She was sobbing with rage, almost unintelligible in her anger.

"You treat me as if I was a servant—patronizing! I hate your beastly way of talking to me! I'm not a dog. I've served you like a slave for twelve years, and I won't be talked to as you talk to me. I won't! I'd sooner starve in the gutter! I suppose I am getting old. I know I am, but you needn't throw it in my face. You're always talking about my looks. If you can't say anything nice, say nothing at all. I'm tired of it."

"Don't be a fool!" scoffed the princess. "And don't be hysterical. You've got your future to consider and you're not going to help by quarrelling with me. You can't go back to the chorus."

"That's the sort of horrible thing you would say," stormed Greta. "I think you're loathsome! I won't do another stroke of work for you."

She ended in a passion of weak tears, and Anita Bellini did not attempt to mollify her. She knew from past experience that in an hour or two she would have a penitent message from her slave asking forgiveness for this outburst; for this was not the first time that Greta had revolted, only to come to heel at the snap of Anita's whip.

With this assurance she took her ungracious leave, and had hardly left the street before all thought of Greta was out of her mind. The Princess Anita Bellini had other matters, more weighty, to think of.

———————————◦———————————

There was very little for Leslie Maughan to tell to her chief, but he did not seem greatly disappointed.

"We'll leave her alone for a while. If you once start badgering these people, they build up an unbreakable alibi, and that's bad for trade."

He looked glumly at the trunks in the corner of his room.

"We'd better dispose of these," he said. "I'll get in a clerk to write down the inventory as you call them out."

He rang for his secretary, the girl who had taken Leslie Maughan's place on her promotion, and, stooping before the first of the cabin trunks, he unlocked it and threw back the lid. For half an hour Leslie was lifting out articles of wearing apparel, and one little mystery was solved when she came upon a parcel of men's clothing. They were of the ready-to-wear type, the parts roughly tacked. One of them, however, must have been fitted, for it was partly sewed, and a small tailor's roll in a pocket of the trunk explained how Druze had avoided the embarrassment of a tailor's fitting. She was evidently a good sewing woman, for the half-finished garment was beautifully tailored. There was nothing, however, in the first trunk that threw any light upon the mystery of her death.

The second box held a surprise: it was filled with women's clothing.

"She was going to drop her disguise when she got to the United States," Leslie concluded, and with this view Mr. Coldwell agreed.

At last the second box was emptied, but again there was nothing that could afford the slightest clue.

"There's a suitcase; we only discovered it this morning; it was in the parcels office at Waterloo," said Coldwell.

He opened a cupboard and took out a crocodile skin travelling grip and put it on the table. It was locked, but suitcase locks respond to almost any key, and at the second attempt it was opened. Here the girl found such articles as she would expect an ocean traveller to carry: sponge bag, soap, a small jewel case containing a gold watch and guard, a diamond-encircled wrist watch, and a small diamond bar brooch. A silk dressing gown, a pair of slippers, and a few odds and ends completed the contents.

"Nothing here," said Leslie.

She ran her hand round the silken lining of the case and suddenly her fingers stopped. She felt a thin, oblong package under the silk. Reaching out, she took Coldwell's scissors from his desk and cut through the silk. Inserting her fingers, she drew forth an envelope. It was closed and bore no inscription. She tore off the end and drew out an oblong document. It was a marriage certificate, performed apparently by the Reverend H. Hermitz, of Elfield, Connecticut.

"Good heavens!" said the startled Coldwell, reading over her shoulder.

For a moment the words swam before the eyes of the girl, and then out of the blur they appeared with staggering clearness. It was a document certifying that Peter James Dawlish had been joined in holy matrimony with Jane Winifred Hood—and Hood was Lady Raytham's maiden name!

She read it again, then put the document into the inspector's hands.

"Then they were married!" she said evenly. "That was the thing I wasn't sure about."

CHAPTER XII.
PETER'S MOTHER

Peter found it very difficult to concentrate his mind upon his work, and although his task was purely mechanical he stopped from time to time and allowed his thoughts to wander. Inevitably they wandered toward that gray building on the Thames Embankment, and a room somewhere in its dark interior where a girl was sitting. He could see her face very clearly. He sighed and took up his pen again, and cursed himself for the folly of dreams.

Far better for him, he thought, that, if he could not concentrate upon his work, he let his mind go roving westward to the bleak moor and those ugly prison buildings that are set in a fold of it; to the carved sneer on the stone arch under which he had walked heavy-footed toward the golden-bearded warder who stood by the iron gates and counted the prisoners in and out; to the long, smelly "ward," and the vaultlike cells with their gayly coloured blankets; to the stretch of bog land from which the convict workers returned soaked to the skin to their lukewarm dinners; to the barnlike laundry, the silent punishment cells, and the cracked asphalt where the prisoners walked in a ring on Sunday mornings. An ugly memory, but at least one of accomplishment, and substantially past. It was much better than letting your fancies go straying toward the straight figure of a girl with violet eyes and red lips that curved everlastingly in laughter.

He had reached the S's in the list, the Simpsons and Sims and Sinclairs. It was ill-paid work, his employer being a bookmaker of dubious probity; but so far as he was concerned, he had been paid something in advance, and he had been promised another job to follow.

Very resolutely he had dismissed from his mind all thought of his mother. Even in Dartmoor he had excluded her from his thoughts. If he remembered at all, it was by the letter that had come to him on the day of his conviction. His father had died that week; he had been sinking for months and had never been conscious of his son's shame. That had been Peter's one comfort, until he received his mother's letter, telling him that in a lucid hour of consciousness old Donald Dawlish had struck his name from his will. So Peter went down from the dock with the bitterness of death in his heart; beside that knowledge of his father's last act, the seven years' sentence was as nothing.

At six o'clock Elizabeth brought him his tea. She was unusually solemn and silent, and when he attempted to start a little conversation with her, she was so embarrassed that he did not attempt to pursue this course.

He went out for an hour, strolling through the Lambeth Cut amid a medley of hawkers' stalls with their glaring acetylene lights. He had some comfort from this contact with his fellows. As he returned, he was opening the door of the house with a key which the woman had given him that day, when he remembered that he had not seen Mrs. Inglethorne since the visitation of the police.

He went upstairs, lit the oil lamp and, putting a paper bag full of biscuits which he had bought on the table before him, he settled down to his task. Eight o'clock was striking when he heard the squeaking of brakes as a motor car stopped before the door, and, going to the window, he pulled aside the shade and looked down. It was too dark to distinguish the visitor, but his heart leaped at the thought that it might be Leslie Maughan and he opened the door and waited. This time he heard Mrs. Inglethorne's voice and after a while she called up to him sourly:

"A lady to see you, Mr. Dawlish."

"Will you ask her to come up, please?"

He went back into the room and waited. The step on the stairs was slower and heavier than Leslie's. And then there came through the open doorway the last woman in the world he expected to see—his mother.

Her cold eyes went from him to the littered table.

"Fine work for the son of a gentleman!" she said in a hard voice.

"I've known worse," he replied coolly.

She closed the door behind her, as though she knew something of Mrs. Inglethorne's irrepressible curiosity.

"I never expected I should see you again," she said, declining with a gesture the chair he pushed forward to her; "but having given the matter a great deal of thought, I have decided that I ought to do something for you. I am buying and stocking a small farm for you in western Canada, and I am making you a small allowance to enable you to live, even if the farm fails, as it probably will. You will leave for Quebec on Saturday week; I have booked a second-class passage for you."

And, when he was about to speak:

"I don't want you to thank me. I shall feel happier when you have left the country. You have brought everlasting disgrace upon your father's name, and I do not wish to be reminded constantly of the fact."

Here she stopped.

"You were altogether wrong when you thought I was about to thank you," he said quietly. "In the first place, I have no intention of accepting your charity, and in the second place I have no aptitude for farming either in Canada or in England."

"I have booked your passage," she said, with an air of finality.

"Then there will be a vacant bed going cheap on the Atlantic Ocean!" replied Peter, with a smile.

She looked round the room contemptuously and again her eyes went to the table.

"So you'd rather do this waster's work?"

"Waster's work, I agree," he said, "but infinitely more intellectual than mending boots or washing convicts' laundry—my last occupation. I expect nothing from you, Mother. For some reason which I have never quite understood, you have hated me ever since I was a child. I have no wish to reproach you with being 'unnatural.' You have been under the thumb of Anita Bellini ever since I can remember."

"How dare you!" Her voice was vibrant with anger. " 'Under the thumb!' What do you mean?"

"I only know that Anita Bellini has withered every good feeling in every good woman who has been brought into contact with her. I only know that she is evil; what hold she has over you, Heaven knows. It has been sufficiently strong to rob me of the one gift which is every man's right—a mother's love. I dare say that sounds a piece of sickly sentimentality, but it is a big thing—a very big thing."

"You have had what you deserved," she interrupted brusquely. "And I did not come here to discuss my duty. If you prefer to go to Australia instead of Canada—"

"I prefer Lambeth to either place at the moment," he said coldly.

She shrugged her shoulders ever so slightly.

"You have made your bed and you must lie on it. I have done all that is humanly possible, more than could be expected, remembering how you have humiliated me and made my name—"

"My father's name," he corrected.

He got under her guard there, and to his wonder the comment to which irritation drove him produced a remarkable effect. Her face flushed; the hard mouth grew harder.

"Your father's name is my name," she said harshly.

Her eyes were blazing; he had never seen her so moved.

"I will give you twenty thousand pounds to leave the country," she said. "That is my final offer."

He shook his head.

"I shall never want money from you," he said, and, walking to the door, opened it and she left the room without another glance at him.

Why had she come? He wasted half an hour of precious time puzzling over this extraordinary action on her part. He had spoken no more than the truth, when he had said that from his childhood she had displayed an antagonism toward him which in maturity had puzzled him more than any other experience in his life. Antagonistic? She hated him! And, curiously enough, his father had known of her feeling, and though he had never made any direct reference to the enmity, had gone out of his way to make up for the affection the mother denied him. It was his father with whom he had corresponded throughout the days of the war; his father who had met him when he came home from France on leave; his father who had come day after day to the hospital to sit by the bedside of his wounded son; and when Peter had been discharged from the army, it was Donald who found him the secretaryship and had planned for him a great career in the world of politics. It was a puzzle beyond unravelment. Peter took up his pen again and tried, by a concentration of his exigent present, to forget the bitter past.

CHAPTER XIII.
PETER TELLS

It was twelve o'clock when he put down his pen and rubbed his cramped hands. Throwing up the window to let out the smoke, he munched a biscuit and meditated; and then his face brightened, and his thoughts went unresistingly toward Leslie Maughan. Then through the open window he heard unsteady steps coming along the paved sidewalk. They paused before the door of the house; there was a rattle of the key. When Mrs. Inglethorne went out at night, she usually returned with that same unsteady footstep. Presently the door slammed, and her muttering came up to him from the passage.

Usually she did not go out nights, but stayed at home to receive the curious callers who came at odd moments. They always knocked once with the knocker and once with the flat of their hands, and generally they carried a parcel or package, big or small. There was a whispered colloquy in the passage, the chink of money, or, more rarely, the rustle of treasury notes, and they went out again—without their parcels. This, Peter had seen and had not seen. Prison had taught him the wisdom of blindness, and he had not spoken to Mrs. Inglethorne of the furtive men and women who came slinking down Severall Street at those hours when the police patrol was well out of the way.

Leslie Maughan! He smiled a little at the thought of her, more at his own madness. What barriers separated them—barriers more real, more invincible, than the difference between Scotland Yard and Dartmoor Prison! It was worse than madness to think about her!

The scream that brought him to his feet was shrill and charged with fear and mortal agony. In two strides he was at the door and had pulled it wide open.

Now he heard it plainly—the whistle and fall of a whip, the terrified, frantic cries for mercy. He ran down the stairs in the dark and tapped at Mrs. Inglethorne's door. From inside the room came a deep, heartbreaking sound of sobbing.

"Who's that?" asked Mrs. Inglethorne defiantly. "Go away and mind your own business!"

"Open the door, or I'll break it open!" cried Peter in a cold fury.

"I'll send for the police if you interfere with me!" yelled the woman.

His answer was to throw his weight against the flimsy door. The catch broke with a snap, and he was in the foul bedroom. Elizabeth lay cowering on a filthy camp bed, clad only in a coarse nightdress. Her head was pillowed in the crook of her arm, and convulsive sobs shook the thin shoulders. Her face aflame, Mrs. Inglethorne stood at the foot of a big brass bedstead, one hand holding herself steady, the other grasping an old dog whip.

"I'll learn her to go talking about me!" she said thickly. "After all I've done for her!"

There was another child there, a girl who was apparently the same age as Elizabeth. She, however, enjoyed the luxury of Mrs. Inglethorne's ample bed and was so used to this exhibition of the woman's wrath that she was asleep.

"Where is your coat, Elizabeth?" asked Peter gently.

The child looked up, her eyes swollen, her face red, and cast one fearful glance at her mother.

"Watcher goin' to do?" asked Mrs. Inglethorne unsteadily.

"She will sleep in my room for the night," replied Peter. "To-morrow I will make other arrangements for her, and if you give any trouble I shall send for the police."

Mrs. Inglethorne was amused in her way.

"Send for the police!" she scoffed. "I like that! An old lag sending for the police! And they'll come, won't they?"

"I think so," said Peter quietly. "They will come, if only to discover why you never use the back room upstairs as a bedroom, why it is always kept locked, except after your visitors' calls."

The smile died from the woman's face.

"As far as I'm concerned," Peter went on, "you can 'fence' till the cows come home! But I'm not going to have you beating this child while I'm in the house. And when I'm out of it, and out of it for good, I'll see that she is well looked after!"

The woman's face was mottled with fear.

"Fence!" she spluttered. "I don't know what you mean by that low word! If you mean I receive stolen property, then you're a liar!"

"Let me call the police and settle the matter," said Peter.

The threat sobered her.

"I don't want any police in my house. The kid annoyed me, and it's a hard thing if a mother can't cane her own children without being interfered with. If she wants to sleep upstairs, she can, but she'd be better off down here, Mr. Dawlish. You haven't got any accommodation for a little gel."

This was true.

"All right, get into bed, Elizabeth." He covered her up with the pitifully thin bedclothes, and without apology took Mrs. Inglethorne's heavy coat that lay over the bed rail and put it on top. "Sleep well," he said, and patted her cheek.

She was safe for the night. What happened in the morning depended entirely on the view which Leslie Maughan took of a scheme that was beginning to take definite shape.

Mrs. Inglethorne was a fence, a buyer of stolen property. He had lived too long in association with the worst criminals of England to have any doubt upon the point, and, squinting through the keyhole one day in his curiosity, he had seen enough to remove the last remnants of doubt that remained.

He went to bed, determined to interview Leslie at the earliest opportunity, and it was not only on Elizabeth's account that the thought pleased him.

When he arrived at the flat in Charing Cross Road next morning, Lucretia did not recognize him, and scowled fearfully at the suggestion that he should be admitted. She looked at his shabby attire and shook her head.

"It's no good your trying to see Miss Maughan. You'd better call on her at Scotland Yard. She's very busy now."

"Who is it, Lucretia?"

Leslie was leaning over the rails of the landing; she could not see the visitor, but she could hear the uncompromising note in Lucretia's voice.

"A young man wants to see you, miss. What's your name again? Dawlish."

"Oh, is that you, Peter Dawlish? Come up, will you?"

Peter ran up the stairs, followed by the muttered protests of the maid.

"You're in time for breakfast. How are the envelopes going?"

"They're melting!" he said.

He was conscious of a certain indefinable change in her tone. It was not that she was more serious, but there seemed some listlessness about her, as though she were tired. It was almost an effort to talk. She looked weary, he saw, when they passed from the dark landing, and he commented on this.

"I've been up half the night," she said, "wandering about in a very cold garden, watching an elderly lady searching the ground with an electric lamp. That sounds mysterious, doesn't it?"

She pointed to a chair and Peter sat down.

"It sounds almost romantic. Where was this?"

"At Wimbledon." She waved the matter out of discussion. "Well," she asked, "what brings you to West Central London at this unholy hour?"

Her grave eyes were fixed on his; there was something of reproach in them, something of hurt. He was puzzled; he felt that he had fallen short in her estimation, that she was disappointed with him for some reason. So strong was this impression that he grew uncomfortable under her gaze, and as though she were aware of this, she dropped her eyes to the table and began slowly to stir her coffee.

"I've come on a fool errand, with a wild and impossible suggestion."

And then he told her of what had happened overnight, of the merciless flogging which Mrs. Inglethorne had administered.

"The woman is a fence," he said, "not in a very big way. I think she specializes in furs and silk lengths."

She knew something of the genus fence, but he told her what he had learned in Dartmoor, of fences who visited the scene of prospective robberies and priced the loot, practically paying for it, before it was stolen; of skillful men and women who would stand outside a small jeweller's shop and with one comprehensive glance assess the thieving value of the whole. He told her of "dead" stores—stores which were locked up at night, where nobody lived on the premises, and of "live" stores, where there was either a watchman or a proprietor and his family sleeping on the floors above.

"I am not reporting this officially—I mean the fence part of it—but the child is ill-used. The other little kids get a whacking now and again, but I should think she gets hers all the time."

"What do you wish me to do?" she asked, looking up at him.

"I don't know." He had a sense of awkwardness. "I had a wild idea that possibly you might be able to find—to do something with her."

"You mean take charge of her?"

She was smiling at him.

"Yes, I suppose I did mean that," he said after a second's thought. "It sounds fantastic and impossible now, but Elizabeth has got a grip on me. Probably it is my own rather unhappy childhood which is responding to her wretchedness."

She laughed.

"I'll make your mind easy, at any rate," she said. "I had already considered the possibility. In fact, I discussed the matter with Lucretia last night before I went out to dinner, and Lucretia was wildly enthusiastic. I have a spare room here; she could go to the Catholic school in Leicester Square. The only point is that we get Mrs. Inglethorne's consent."

"She had better," he said grimly, and her lips twitched.

"Really, you're almost ferocious when you're taking up the causes of other people," she said. "I wish you'd be a little energetic in your own."

"Aren't I?"

She shook her head.

"Not very," she answered, in her quiet way. "Why don't you see your mother?"

He grinned.

"She saved me the trouble and came last night."

"To Severall Street?" she asked in astonishment, and when he nodded: "Was it—a pleasant—encounter?"

"A normally strained interview," he answered cheerfully. "She endeavoured to instill in me a passion for agriculture, and Canadian agriculture at that. I love Canada. You can't even take a week-end trip into Canada without loving it. But the prospect of milking cows in Saskatchewan didn't appeal."

"She wanted you to go abroad? Why?"

He shrugged his shoulders.

"I suppose she rather feels there isn't room enough for both of us in London."

She thought the matter over for a minute.

"Didn't your father leave you any money?"

"He cut me off without the proverbial shilling."

The lightness of his tone, she suspected, was assumed. Coldwell had told her how much Peter had loved his father.

"He altered his will at the eleventh hour—the day before I was sentenced—and left me nothing. Poor old dear! I haven't the slightest grudge. How could I? He was the best father that ever lived."

She had said she rarely smoked; she took a cigarette from her bag now and lit it without looking at him. Indeed, for the next four minutes, as he talked about his envelope addressing and his future, it seemed that she was more interested in the blue vapour that floated from the end of her cigarette than in his narrative.

"You're unfortunate."

She put down the cigarette, carefully took out a spoonful of coffee from the cup and dropped it on the glowing end as it lay in the saucer.

"You're unfortunate, Peter Dawlish, both as a son—and as a husband!"

He did not speak.

"Terribly unfortunate," she went on moodily. "I think you must have been born under a very unlucky star. I'm not asking you for confidences; you'd hate me if I did."

Presently:

"How did you know?"

She fetched a long sigh.

"How did I know? Oh, I only knew yesterday for sure. I'd guessed for a long time—ever since I went on my holidays into Cumberland and found a little volume of Elizabeth Barrett Browning's with an inscription in doggerel blank verse on the fly leaf. It was when I saw that the first letter of every line reading from below, upward, made the words "Jane Hood" that I first guessed. But I wasn't certain—about the marriage. There was no record at Somerset House."

"We were married in America."

She nodded.

"I know that now; but why?"

He stared past her out of the window. Here, she thought, was a man who really regarded life as a terribly serious business. She was mighty glad of that.

"Jane was very unhappy at home; her people were rotten. Her father kept a gambling house, and her mother—" He shrugged. "I fell in love with her. If I hadn't been a fool I would have gone to my father and told him the truth and then, in all probability, there would have been no cause for unhappiness. But I was aware that he knew Jane's people and knew that they were rotten. We went away to America together and were married in a little town in Connecticut. I suppose you know that? Her father was American born. From the first day the marriage was a ghastly mistake. Jane thought I had unlimited money. I had to pawn her jewels to get home, and there was a fearful scene when we landed at Liverpool. We were both a little crazy, and agreed then and there to separate. I went back to Lord Everreed's house to find detectives awaiting me at the railway station. I haven't seen or spoken with Jane since."

"Has she divorced you?"

He shook his head.

"I don't know. Things like that are possible in America, but I've had no notification."

Leslie bit her lip.

"If she hasn't, she's committed bigamy. You realize that?"

"I realize that," he said shortly. "Which means that I cannot free myself without betraying her; I can't do that. I couldn't expose her to imprisonment."

There was a tense and painful silence.

"Is that all?" she asked. "All you have to tell me?"

"You did not need telling, I think," he said, a little bitterly.

"No." She lit another cigarette; the flame of the match quivered unsteadily. "You're very unfortunate, Peter Dawlish."

She blew out the match with deliberation and put it carefully in her saucer by the side of the sodden cigarette.

"You knew nothing about Druze, of course, or you would have told me. When did you say your father disinherited you?"

"The day before I went to prison."

She considered this.

"Tell me, Peter! You don't mind my calling you Peter? I feel rather sisterly toward you just now. What was the relationship between your father and mother? Cordial?"

He shook his head.

"No, they were never cordial; they were polite."

She bit her lip, looking at him absently.

"Did you ever see the Princess Bellini at your father's house?"

"Only once," he replied. "Father disliked her—"

"She was a sort of aunt, wasn't she?" Leslie interrupted.

"I've never exactly fathomed the relationship. I've always understood that the Princess Bellini's brother married my mother's sister."

She rose from the table abruptly, for no apparent reason.

"Peter Dawlish," she said, and her voice shook a little in spite of her assumption of banter, "if you were cursed with my intense curiosity you might be a very much happier man."

"What do you mean?" he asked.

"I'll tell you—some day. And now let us get back to our muttons; and our muttons for the moment is poor Elizabeth. The only difficulty in the way is Mrs. Inglethorne. As a loving mother, she may very well object to her child being taken from her. Obviously I cannot use the same argument as you have used. If she is a fence and a lawbreaker, it is my duty to inform Mr. Coldwell and have her arrested. If she isn't a lawbreaker, we shall have to get after her from another angle. That sounds terribly businesslike. I think I'll go back with you to Severall Street and see Mrs. Inglethorne myself. She may be amenable to reason."

CHAPTER XIV.
AN ARREST

They went by bus to the southern end of Westminster Bridge and walked along York Road together. Just before they reached Severall Street they saw a small motor truck turn into the main road, and mechanically, Leslie, who had a weakness for such mental registrations, turned her head to note the number. It was a favourite trick of hers to carry fifty or sixty motor-car numbers in her head and jot them down at the close of the day—a practice into which Mr. Coldwell had initiated her. As she looked round she heard:

"Lady!"

A shrill voice called her.

"Who was that?" she asked, but Peter had not heard.

They reached the house and he opened the door and called Mrs. Inglethorne, but it was one of the children who answered.

"Mother's gone out. Her and Elizabeth."

Sometimes the woman took the child with her when she went shopping, Peter explained.

"I'm afraid I've brought you on a long job," he said. "She may be out for hours."

Leaving her for a moment in the passage, he ran upstairs to his room, intending to show her one of his small treasures, the photograph of his dead father. He reached the head of the stairs and then stopped aghast. The door of the mysterious locked room which adjoined his own was wide open, and when he strode in he saw it was empty. Mrs. Inglethorne was a quick worker, and, in the space of time between his departure and his return, had removed all evidence of her guilt.

He went into his own room, pulled open the drawer of the table where he kept his few treasures, and had taken out the small leather-covered portfolio when he saw some writing on the pad—a few scribbled words in a childish hand: "She has taken me away. Elizabeth."

He tore off the corner of the blotting paper and went back to the girl.

"I was afraid of this," she said in a low voice. "Do you remember the cry 'lady' as we passed the motor van? Where is the nearest telephone booth?"

At the corner of the street was a little general shop, which had a telephone sign, and Leslie almost ran to the shop. There was some delay before the instrument was disengaged, but in a few minutes she was connected with Scotland Yard and was talking to Coldwell.

"The number of the car is X.Y. 63369," she said. "There is no doubt whatever that it contains stolen property, but it is the little girl I want."

"I'll send out a call," was Coldwell's reply. "We may not pick it up before to-night; on the other hand, we may be lucky."

"Where are you going now?" asked Peter when they were outside the shop.

"Back to the house," said Leslie. "I want to look at that room."

"They cleared everything."

She nodded.

"Thieves in a hurry are very careless people, and perhaps Mrs. Inglethorne isn't so clever as she imagines."

The room was apparently bare; the only article of furniture it contained was a long table, and by the dust marks on this Leslie was able to judge the extent of the property that had been stored. On either side of the rusty fireplace was a cupboard. One of these she opened and found empty, except for a little heap of rubbish at the bottom. The second, however, was locked. With a table knife borrowed from the kitchen she forced back the catch and pulled open the door. There was nothing very much there, but enough. There were three bolts of silk, one still bearing the label of the wholesaler from whom it had been stolen.

"Thieves in a hurry are very careless," she said, with the light of battle in her eyes, "and it really doesn't matter whether Mrs. Inglethorne is hanged for a sheep or a lamb, so long as she's well and truly hanged!"

She sent Peter to the police station, and went down to interview the children. A grubby lot of little people they were, very pale, very starved looking, except one who apparently was in charge in Mrs. Inglethorne's absence. She was the little girl, Leslie learned later, who had slept in the woman's bed, and, unlike the others, she bore a striking facial resemblance to her mother.

"You didn't find nothing, did you?" She was frankly hostile. "You've got to be up very early to catch my old woman, missis!"

And then, turning to the silent semi-circle of children who constituted the remainder of Mrs. Inglethorne's family, she ordered them peremptorily away.

"Go and play in the back yard."

Poor little starvelings! Leslie's heart ached to see them. She sought, by delicate inquiry, to discover where Elizabeth had been taken, but the preternatural cunning of the child she questioned baffled her.

Peter came back in a very short time, accompanied by a uniformed inspector and a plain-clothes officer. They made an inspection of the silk and carried it off with them to the station.

"This may affect you a little, Peter Dawlish," said Leslie when they were alone. "The children will be removed to the workhouse this afternoon, and Mrs. Inglethorne will be arrested immediately on her return, so that you will have the house to yourself."

He laughed.

"I'm not depressed," he said.

He walked with her as far as Westminster Bridge Road, and at parting she asked him a curious question.

"What would you do if you had half a million pounds?"

He looked at her in astonishment and laughed.

"That isn't my favourite dream," he said. "But I think the first thing I should do would be to send to America to discover whether I have been, as you would say, 'well and truly' divorced."

"Indeed?" Her tone was a trifle cold. "Is that necessary when Jane Raytham is within a penny bus ride?"

And with a nod she was gone.

Peter returned to the house and found it very difficult to resume his work or concentrate his mind upon lists. He had hardly started before the police officials came with an omnibus to take away the children, and they departed with no visible reluctance, except in the case of the girl whom Leslie had interviewed.

At four o'clock in the afternoon Mrs. Inglethorne came into the house in triumph, and without going into the kitchen mounted the stairs and stood, arms akimbo, her red face made hideous by a self-satisfied smirk, confronting her lodger.

"Well, did you bring in the police?" she demanded. "And what are you going to do with Elizabeth?" And, when he did not answer, she shook her fist at him. "Out you go, out of my house, you police informer. I'll learn you to go prying around and threatening me! You leave this room at once or I'll send for a policeman."

"I think I'll stay," he said good-humouredly.

"Oh, will you?"

She went to the door and called:

"Emma."

There was no answer.

"I can save you a lot of trouble, Mrs. Inglethorne," said Peter, putting down his pen. "Your children have been taken away to the workhouse."

She staggered back against the wall, her big mouth open wide.

"W-why?" she stammered.

"It is usual to take children to the workhouse when their parents are arrested and there are no other relatives to look after them," he said.

"Arrested?" she screamed.

He nodded to the window, and she staggered past him and, pulling up the sash, looked out. Two men were standing on the opposite sidewalk, and one nodded as to an old friend. She recognized the detective sergeant who had arrested her husband.

"They can't touch me!" she screamed. "They can't touch me! It's my word against yours—"

"Unfortunately you left a few bolts of silk behind in the cupboard," answered Peter.

Mrs. Inglethorne was in a state of collapse when the detectives came in to arrest her.

The motor truck had been traced; the driver and a man who accompanied the car had been driven to the nearest police station, where the plunder was checked and exhibited in preparation for the charge which would follow. They either could not or would not, however, give any information concerning the child, and when Leslie went to Lambeth to interview Mrs. Inglethorne in her cell, she was no more successful.

"Find her!" rapped the woman. "She's in good hands, that's where she is. I'm not saying anything. If you want her, find her! That's my last word to you!"

Leslie did not notify Peter that she was coming to Lambeth. Passing up Severall Street on her way home, she saw the light in the upstairs window and guessed that he was still working hard. A postman rapped at the door, and she waited a while until it was opened, as she guessed, by Peter, and almost turned back just to say a word to him. And if she overcame this deplorable weakness, it was not lightly done.

"Leslie Maughan," she said to herself, mounting the steps of Hungerford Bridge, "do you know what you are doing? Shall I tell you in the vulgarest terms? You're chasing a married man! Leslie, that isn't done! Not in the best society."

She was uncommonly weary when she dragged herself into her own sitting room, deciding to forgo the duty she had planned. This was a second call upon

Greta Gurden. That afternoon there had been a consultation at Scotland Yard, but matters had not developed sufficiently to justify the issue even of a search warrant.

After a light dinner she took out the letter she had received two nights before, spread the foolscap on her desk and examined it carefully. It was a queer story she read, even in the stilted terminology of an elderly country parson, who employed such words as "primogeniture," and felt it necessary to sprinkle his pages with quotations from Horace, mostly in Latin. The writer was the vicar of a small Devonshire parish near Budleigh Salterton, and he had, as he said in a preliminary flourish, "reached the fourscore of the prophet." He wasted a page in explaining how he came to reach these years, and employed *"mens sana in corpore sano"* at least twice in the first folio.

He knew the Druze family very well; they lived in his village and had done so for hundreds of years. He himself had baptized Alice Mary Druze and Annie Emily Druze, and several other members of the Druze family which he thought it was necessary to enumerate by their full names; it had necessitated long researches in ancient registers. The Druze family had for generations farmed some forty acres of poor land on the edge of Dartmoor. They were "a wild family with a bad history," and here the reverend gentleman, who was also something of a scientist, branched away from the main track to a discourse upon heredity which would have done credit to a Lombroso.

Old father Druze was a lunatic and had died mad; his grandfather had committed suicide; there was a record in the parish registry and a note that he had been buried at the crossroads, in the proper manner for such as take their lives; Druze's grandmother had also a history of sorts. The clergyman remembered her as a "respectable woman," though inclined to gayety, and he even felt it necessary to retail a hundred-year-old piece of scandal, something that had happened at Widdicombe Fair.

Alice was illiterate; he had extracted a note of this fact from the register of the church school. Annie, on the other hand, was a diligent scholar "and showed surprising proficiency in the study of the so-called dead languages," so that she "speedily secured a respectable situation with a haberdasher in Exeter, a Mr. Watson. She was a God-fearing young woman, a communicant, and eventually married a well-to-do farmer in the neighbourhood of Torquay." The farmer's name Leslie jotted down on her pad.

The third of the daughters, Martha, was of an "exemplary character, though of no great educational attainments." About her the clergyman was very explicit, for it was he who had obtained her a post first as stillroom maid at a Plymouth hospital, and afterward, on his recommendation, as a probationary nurse. It was believed that she went to South Africa and "married a prosperous carpenter."

When Leslie had traced Druze to that little Devonshire village, and wrote, with no great hope, to the vicar, she hardly expected so voluminous and conscientious a record of the family history; for he even sent photographs of tombstones which marked the departed Druzes of the Eighteenth Century!

If she had only read this before, she thought, she could not have been shocked by the discovery that "Arthur Druze" was a woman; for apparently there was no male member in that family, except the semi-lunatic father and a remote uncle who for some reason wasn't called Druze at all. She read through carefully, took down an atlas and a gazetteer from her bookshelf, and finally locked letter and data in the drawer. Her work was by no means finished for the night, though she was dropping with weariness. She had a number of letters to write. Before she had left the office, Mr. Coldwell had given her the names and addresses of a dozen people who would be helpful to her in the search she was making.

At eleven o'clock they phoned from Scotland Yard to tell her that there was no news of Elizabeth. Mrs. Inglethorne, confronted as she was with a long term of imprisonment, possibly of penal servitude, refused any information about the child, except that she had gone to "her aunt's."

Lucretia brought her coffee. The girl had an irritating trick of expressing her disapproval by audible tut-tuts, and twice did she tut-tut into the room and out again. At last she extinguished all the lights in the room save the table lamp.

"You've got to go to bed, miss," she said firmly. "I'll have you on my hands if I'm not careful. And what about this young girl?"

Leslie rose stiffly from her desk, gathered the letters together and stamped them.

"She is not coming to-night," she said. "Post these, Lucretia. I'll wait for you to return and then you can go to bed."

She heard the door open and guessed, by the cold draft that swept up the stairs, that Lucretia had followed her usual practice of leaving the door ajar while she went to the nearest pillar-box, which was some distance from the flat.

It was part of the night's routine that Lucretia should take the letters; almost a ritual that Leslie should stand in the open doorway of her sitting room until she heard the girl return.

The maid could not have been gone half a minute before the street door below closed softly. She heard the gentle thud of it.

"Is that you, Lucretia?" she called down into the dark hall.

There was no reply.

Her flesh crept, for no reason that she could understand; a cold shiver went down her spine. Leslie Maughan was not a nervous girl. Her duty and association with Coldwell had taken her into many uncomfortable situations, and unless it was because she was very tired, there was no particular reason for nervousness. But her sensation was something more than the uneasiness which comes to the strongest nerves when they are left alone in a house. It was a premonition, a warning, indeed a certain knowledge that there was somebody in the hall below who should not be there.

She went back into the room, closed the door quietly and slipped in a bolt she had had fitted. She switched on the lights that Lucretia had extinguished, and, going to the window, pulled the curtains apart and lifted the sash. Charing Cross Road was fairly well crowded with people. It was a clear night and a few paces away she saw two policemen patrolling, and presently she discerned Lucretia making her way hurriedly across the road. The maid came beneath the window simultaneously with a policeman; Leslie called her and she looked up.

"Tell the policemen I want them to come in," she said. "Here is the key—catch!"

One of the officers caught the key deftly.

"Anything wrong, miss?" he asked, knowing her.

"I think somebody has come into the house while my maid went out to post a letter. You left the door open, did you, Lucretia?"

"Yes, miss, I did," confessed the agitated Lucretia. "I forgot to take the key."

"Well, hurry—" she began.

At that moment all the lights in the room went out.

She sat on the sill and swung out her legs, her eyes fixed on the door, which was visible in the light of a street lamp. A faint creaking sound came to her ears and she saw the door move slightly—the bolt was straining under some enormous pressure. Then a voice from the pavement below hailed her.

"The street door won't open, miss," said the policeman's voice.

She looked back at the door. The slot of the bolt was giving under the strain.

"Can you catch me?" she asked.

The two men ran to the pavement beneath her.

"Jump!"

Again she looked back. At that moment, with a crash, the door opened. She had a dim vision of two stunted figures, then, bracing her hands on the sill, she jumped.

It was not a dignified landing, but for the moment Leslie Maughan was less interested in her dignity than her safety. A crowd had already gathered, attracted by the unusual happening, and there appeared from nowhere an inspector of police, a resourceful man who, having heard the story, immediately stopped an omnibus and ordered the driver to bring his big machine onto the sidewalk immediately beneath the window. Standing on the rail of the bus, one of the policemen reached the window sill and climbed inside, and was followed by the inspector. There was no sound of the struggle which the morbid crowd expected. A few minutes later the door below was unbolted and Leslie and the trembling Lucretia went into the passage.

They found the hall window on the first landing wide open. A police whistle buzzed in the street; in a very short time the block would be surrounded.

"No, they haven't cut the wire, as far as I can see," said the inspector, examining the wall of the passage with his lamp. "Where do you keep your fuse box?"

"I think it is near the door," said the girl.

It proved to be within easy reach. The flat had been darkened by the simple expedient of removing the fuses. They found them intact on the floor and replaced them, and an inspection was possible. Except for the broken door, no damage had been done to the flat. Whoever the intruders were, their time had been too short to conduct a search of the room. The drawers of the desk were untouched.

"They hadn't much time, had they?" said the puzzled inspector. "I can't understand this job. If they were ordinary burglars they would have cleared just as soon as they knew you had spotted them."

Half an hour later, and before the police had departed, Mr. Coldwell came on the scene. By this time every roof and yard in the vicinity had been searched; night watchmen had been aroused from their surreptitious sleep, and a small army of police detectives had examined every window that might afford a possible means of escape. But no sign of the intruders was discovered.

"I don't like this," said Leslie.

Mr. Coldwell shook his head.

"You'll have to find other lodgings for a while. To-morrow you had better transfer your belongings and Lucretia to my house at Hampstead."

For five minutes he discussed in a low voice the theories he had formed, the plans he had made.

"I don't think it is necessary to leave a policeman in the house," he said at last, and a little yellow man curled up on the top of the high bureau in Leslie's room, screened from observation by the old-fashioned frieze of the wardrobe, was relieved.

He heard the policemen go clattering down the stairs, and after a while:

"Just phone me if you're at all nervous, Leslie. Good-night."

Coldwell's voice sounded from the hall; there was the slam of a door. The little yellow man, who spoke and understood English very well, did not smile to himself, because he was of a race that seldom smile.

Leslie went into her bedroom with a yawn, gathered her sleeping things and disappeared into the bathroom. The listener heard the sound of running water, heard her bid a reassuring good-night to the tremulous servant, and then the door of the bedroom opened and closed. The light was extinguished; there was the creak of a bed, and after a while the sound of deep, regular breathing.

For an hour the yellow man lay, not moving a muscle, and then, reaching up, he caught hold of the wooden moulding, tested its strength, and was satisfied. He felt the long, queer-shaped knife that was in his belt, and, with the agility of a cat, and supported only by his sinewy fingers, he drew himself clear of the wardrobe, and dropped noiselessly on to the carpet.

The wardrobe hardly creaked as he moved; save for the soft pad of his bare feet and the breathing of the sleeper there was no sound. Holding the knife lightly in his right hand, he groped along the pillow with his left, ready to pounce upon and strangle the scream before it rose.

There was no head on the first pillow, none on the right—the bed was empty. He straightened himself up quickly, half turned as he heard a sound from behind him, but it was too late. An arm of steel flung round his throat, the knife hand was gripped at the wrist and twisted so sharply that the weapon fell to the floor.

"I want you!" It was Coldwell's voice.

He lifted the little figure without difficulty, and reached out his hand to turn on the light. At that moment the prisoner recovered himself, and with amazing strength twisted round to face the detective. Coldwell realized that he had on his hands something with the ferocity and suppleness of a wild cat, something that growled and clawed and kicked so that not a limb of him was still. The unexpectedness of that furious onslaught threw him for a second off his balance. He drove out with his right, but as though he could see in the dark, the assassin dodged, and in another second he was free and had flown through the open door. Coldwell followed, but too late. With one leap the little man crashed through sash and pane and dropped unharmed to the street below. A policeman made a dive at him, but he ducked, flew across the road, and disappeared down a court by the side of a theatre toward St. Martin's Lane.

"Didn't even see him," said Coldwell bitterly, when he called the girl in from Lucretia's room. The detective's face was scratched, his collar torn. "It was rather like tackling a young tiger."

Leslie had turned on the lights and they saw the extent of the damage. He must have dived for the lower sash, head-first, for the upper window was untouched. There was not a scrap of glass remaining, and the cross supports of wood were smashed to splinters.

"I've heard of such things being done," said Coldwell, "and I've seen them done—on the stage! But never in real life and through three-quarter inch moulding!"

Leslie was still dressed. She had been waiting in the maid's room, a pistol on her lap, till the sound of the struggle brought her out, just too late. Mr. Coldwell disappeared into the bedroom and returned with the ugly and curious-shaped knife which the man had dropped.

"Eastern," he said, as he felt the edge gingerly. "Malayan, I guess."

He also had been sitting on a chair immediately to the right of the wardrobe, but until he had made an examination later he had not known from what place his assailant had come.

"I thought he'd come back through the window," he mused. "That's one of the curiosities of human nature, Leslie; jot it down in your notebook. We always look *under* things for hidden criminals; we never look over; and yet the cleverest fellow that ever got away from the police was a steeplejack who hid for a fortnight at the top of a smokestack! Ever wear garters, Leslie?"

She laughed softly.

"That almost sounds indelicate to me," she said. "No, I won't go very deeply into the question, but I don't wear garters!"

He was quite serious.

"Wish you would, just to oblige me. One garter, anyhow. I meant to give it to you to-day."

He drew something out of his pocket and she gasped.

"You really wish me to wear this?"

He nodded.

"A little heavy, but I wish you would," he said.

He insisted upon staying the night, and to make doubly sure had a policeman put on duty in the hall below. Early as the hour was when she went out to her bath, she found him up and dressed, studying the morning newspaper.

"Wonderful how you miss things when you're away from the Yard for a few hours," he drawled.

She turned back from the open door of the bathroom. When Mr. Coldwell drawled, there was something sensational to come.

"What have we missed?" she asked. It was not entirely curiosity which made her ask.

He looked at the newspaper again and took off his glasses.

"Peter Dawlish was arrested last night."

She gazed at him in horror and amazement.

"Arrested? On what charge?"

"Threatening to murder Princess Anita Bellini," was the staggering reply.

CHAPTER XV.
TRAPPED

Rarely did Mrs. Greta Gurden permit herself the luxury of brooding upon her injuries. She was no philosopher, and it was sheer necessity which made her disregard the irritations, petty and great, of life, and concentrate her mind upon pleasant things. But she found herself helpless with a leg that throbbed and throbbed, and the memory of Anita Bellini's insolence rankled as sorely. She was propped up in bed with a heap of papers on her lap. Though there was no immediate need for the work she had taken in hand, and, in truth, sought it only as a relief from boredom, she permitted herself the illusion that she was the victim of a task mistress who was not satisfied with her normal and heavy exactions, but must needs add to her offence this torment of a sick woman.

Old letters, old bills, a receipt or two, a few ancient telegrams about nothing in particular, dozens of letters dealing earnestly with forgotten accounts, an interminable correspondence between Anita and a house agent—she turned the pages one by one, sorting the sheep from the goats.

Presently she came to an old letter typewritten on plain paper—Anita, like her dependent, had used a small portable typewriter for years. The letter was unfinished; halfway through the princess had changed her mind, or probably substituted another for this and had tossed the rejected scrap aside to be gathered to the heap which had accumulated and which was now being sorted.

She read the letter through as far as it went; she was sourly amused. Anita must have been in a careless mood when she threw this away. The old instinct of service told her that it ought to be destroyed at once. She gripped the paper to tear it, thought better of her impulse, and began to consider certain possibilities. To say that she felt bitterly against Anita Bellini at that moment would be to grade her emotion charitably. She was getting old, was she? She had lost her looks and was unlikely to get a job in the chorus. Anita had taken it for granted that she would be forever satisfied with the humiliating position of companion. Capri was to be a kind of bonus.

The princess was a woman of temperament, sometimes feverishly elated, sometimes savagely depressed. Yet in all her permutations of mood, she had been consistently contemptuous of her hireling. Greta grew red and hot and cold at the memory of the insults which this woman had heaped upon her, and the hand that held the letter shook. And then an idea began to take shape in her mind; it was half formed when she called Mrs. Hobbs.

"Get my address book."

She was a systematic woman, and entered without fail the location even of chance acquaintances who might be of no value to her. She ran her thumb down the index till it stopped at "D"; the last entry on the crowded page was "Peter Dawlish."

"Give me an envelope, please, and my fountain pen; and take this letter to the post—no, bring my little typewriter."

The obedient Mrs. Hobbs carried the tiny machine, which was a replica of Anita's, and laid it on the invalid's lap. Greta inserted the envelope, typed the address, and while the instrument was being removed, inserted the torn sheet of paper and licked down the flap of the envelope.

"Go to the general post office—you'd better take a bus each way—and post this. If anybody asks you whether you've posted a letter for me, you're to say no."

It was not the first time Mrs. Hobbs had received similar instructions.

The houses in Severall Street are not equipped with letter boxes, and postmen have learned by experience that inserting letters under doors which are backed by coarse fibre mats is a difficult and sometimes an impossible proposition.

Peter heard the heavy rat-tat of the postman and, going downstairs, opened the door.

"Dawlish?" asked the postman.

"That is my name," said Peter, in surprise. He took the letter and closed the door. Had he followed the practice of Severall Street and its people, which is never to go to the door without making a scrutiny up and down the street, he could not have failed to see Leslie on her way home.

His first thought was that it was a letter from her, but when he brought it to the light of his room, he saw that it was typewritten and had been posted in the city.

He opened the envelope and took out a sheet of typewriting paper. It was discoloured, and one corner had been torn off. He looked at the date and had a mild shock.

"July 7, 1916."

And yet—as he saw—it had been posted that afternoon. There were just three or four lines, the last of which stopped abruptly in the middle of a sentence. Only dimly did he comprehend the significance of the fragment.

> Dear Jane: Druze has found a very good home for your son in a middle-class family. There are no other children. He will be well cared for. And—

Scribbled below in pencil, and almost indecipherable, were the words: "Martha's servant."

He must have read the letter a dozen times before he understood.

"Jane's son—Jane's little son!" He came to his feet slowly, his limbs trembling, the paper swimming before his eyes.

Jane's son—his son! The consciousness of fatherhood momentarily overwhelmed him. Jane had had a child. He had never dreamed—somewhere in the world was a little boy, fatherless—his little boy! He grew hot at the thought. And then, in a frenzy of impatience, he took up his coat, struggled into it, and, not stopping to extinguish the lamp, ran down the stairs and out of the house.

The bus that carried him to Piccadilly seemed to crawl. He got down at a traffic block at Bond Street, half walked, half ran into Berkeley Street, and came at last to the dark portals of Lady Raytham's house. It was past ten. She might be out. But he would wait for her—all night if necessary. He hated her at that moment and there was jealousy behind the hate. He hated her for not telling him, for excluding him from the knowledge and inspiration of their gift. Perhaps he was being brought up as Raytham's child, to call him "father." Peter grew insanely furious at the thought.

To the new butler who opened the door all callers were as yet strange. Peter seemed no stranger than others and he was met civilly.

"What name shall I tell her ladyship?" he asked.

"Mr. Peter," said Peter, after thought.

He was shown into the small drawing room, and paced up and down like a caged animal until he heard the door open and, turning, met face to face, for the first time in eight years, the woman of "the adventure."

She was pale but very calm and sure of herself as she closed the door behind her. For a while they stood, looking at each other. She had matured, grown more beautiful; the old, graceful carriage was unchanged; the enticing lines of her had come to a greater perfection. He had grown older, she thought, was much more of a man than when she had known him before. His face had formed; he had resolution and strength and a balance that had been missing; in his eyes she read something that chilled her.

"You wish to see me, Peter?" she asked.

He nodded.

He was trembling; feared to speak lest his voice betray him.

"What is it you wish to see me about?"

"I want my child." His voice was low; the words seemed to choke him, so that he ended on a cough.

"You want—your child?"

She shook her head so slightly that if he had not been watching her closely the gesture would have escaped him.

"Will you tell me what you mean?"

She was fencing. She wanted time to take all this in. He had shocked her very badly.

"Why pretend, Jane? You know what I want, and what I mean. Where is our child?"

She passed her hand wearily across her eyes.

"I don't know," she said. She made no attempt to evade the question, accepted his knowledge, startling as it was, "I don't know. Is it worth while knowing? He is very happy. I did what was best, Peter. I told nobody. When I went to Reno—"

"You have divorced me?"

She did not answer. A lie trembled on her lips and was instantly rejected—impatiently.

"No, I have not divorced you," she said. "They would not grant me a divorce because you had not been served with the papers—or something of the sort. I don't understand the law very well. I was a fool, of course."

Another intense silence.

"That puts me in your hands, doesn't it?" she went on. "Though I don't imagine you will—"

He stopped her with an impatient gesture.

"I'm not thinking of you and I'm not thinking of myself," he said. "I am thinking of the boy. You don't know? Jane, you horrify me! You don't know where your own child— Good heavens! I thought he might not be here, but that you should tell me so quietly and calmly that you've lost track of him—as if he were a—"

She shook her head.

"I don't know. Honestly, Peter, I don't know. I was terrified when I knew he was coming. I just dimly remember seeing the little thing, and then they took him away—we had arranged it beforehand."

"Who are 'we?' "

She hesitated.

"Anita was very good to me, and so was Druze. It was only then I discovered that Druze was a woman. I had to pay for it afterward—Druze's knowledge, I mean. I don't really remember the child—only just that vague, queer impression like the elusive memory of a dream. Peter, be a little pitiful. I was in a terrible condition; my father was writing, asking me to make up my mind about Raytham. You knew he wanted to marry me? Raytham had lent Father a lot of money, and I was afraid, terribly afraid, of what would happen if Father came to learn—about the marriage and everything.

"He knew I'd been to America, of course; I was supposed to have taken an engagement to sing—you remember that, don't you, Peter? But he didn't know I'd returned, or what had become of me. I had to send all my letters to a friend in New York to be posted back to him."

She stopped.

"Where is the child? That is all I want to know."

She shook her head.

"Druze knew. She told me something just before she went out; she had been drinking, Peter. She told me a ghastly thing." Her voice broke. "Terrible, terrible!" She covered her eyes again, and he waited, his heart a heavy stone.

"This ghastly thing; what was it?" he asked at last.

"She said"—this needed courage to think, it was a torture to say—"that even she didn't know where the child was; that she had handed the boy to the first person who, for a consideration, offered to adopt it; and all the time I had been comforting myself with the thought that—that he at least was being brought up happily, however much a blackguard his foster father was."

"What do you mean?" he demanded.

"I've been paying money, big sums of money," she said at last, "as I supposed to the man who had adopted him, and who, learning of my marriage to Raytham, had for years blackmailed me. Too late I discovered that this blackmailer was mythical, that it was Druze who was robbing me all the time."

Peter drew a deep breath.

"How awful! How perfectly awful!" he whispered. "Just disappeared into the mass—and you allowed him to go. I can't understand that. I thought that women—"

She stopped him with a weary gesture.

"I don't understand women, either. I wish I'd kept him and had faced all the trouble that would have followed. You know about it for the first time, Peter, and you have the support of your righteousness. It has been a bad dream to me—an eight-year long discomfort. And now it is a nightmare." She pressed her throbbing temples. "I can't sleep for thinking of him. That little mite of a boy—my boy and yours—perhaps being starved, or dead perhaps, or suffering—"

She screwed her eyes tight as though to shut out a horrible vision.

"Does Bellini know?" He was like ice now.

"Anita?" She looked at him in surprise. "No; why should she? You hate Anita, of course. I'm not really—fond of her. She's difficult. But she was very helpful to me, Peter."

He looked at her steadily.

"Who was Martha?"

He saw by her frown that she did not understand him.

"Do you know a woman called Martha?"

She shook her head.

"I don't remember anybody of that name. Why?"

"Martha's servant had the child. Bellini knows. And what Bellini knows, I will know."

He made as though to leave the room, but she barred the way.

"Peter, will you forgive me? I've been a fool—a wicked fool, Peter. I'd gladly change places with my own kitchen maid to undo all the past. You loathe me, don't you?"

"No, I don't loathe you," he said quietly. "I'm awfully sorry for you in a way; but I'm disappointed in you, too, Jane. You've been a weakling."

"Have I? I suppose I have." She saw him, a blurred figure, through a mist of tears. "I suppose I have. And one pays dearer for weakness than for wickedness, I think. Where are you going?"

"I'm going to find the child."

She threw out her arms in a gesture of despair.

"Find the child! If you only could! Peter, if you could bring him to me and—"

"You!" He laughed harshly. "The child belongs to me! To me! Do you hear? You had him and lost him. If I find him I will keep him."

He brushed past her, threw open the door, and stalked through the hall into the night.

He had still the greater part of the twenty pounds left that Leslie had given to him, and at this moment of crisis he must spend; he could not afford to economize. A taxi driver accepted with some reluctance his order to drive to Wimbledon Common. It was a long journey, and he had time to put in order the confusion of his mind.

Anita Bellini knew; he was confident of that. And if she knew, he should know. Her residence was a mansion, standing in two acres of ground on the fashionable side of Wimbledon Common; a big, somewhat old-fashioned house, garnished with the square towers and big Gothic turrets which were the joy of the Victorian architects. It had something of a mediæval appearance, seemed to be a veritable castle of despair when he ordered the cab to wait. The cautious man demanded something on account, and wisely, as it proved.

He strode up the gravelled drive. No light showed in any window; even the transom above the massive front door was lifeless. He pulled the bell and the faint clang of it came back to him. After a long time he heard the rattle of chains, the shooting back of a bolt, and a faint light was reflected behind the fanlight. The door was opened a few inches by a very old man with dirty white hair and wearing the slovenly uniform of a footman. Peter saw that the longer chain was still fastened to the door and that the aperture was not big enough to squeeze through.

"You're Simms, aren't you?" He remembered the ancient. "I want to see the princess."

The old man made the grimace that Peter remembered.

"You can't see the princess; she's not at home," he said in a loud cracked voice.

"Tell her Peter Dawlish wishes to see her, and if she will not let me in she can come to the door," he said.

He was not prepared to have the door slammed in his face, yet that was what happened. He waited for five minutes, and then he heard the lock turn. This time he saw Anita. She wore a long green dress, smothered as usual with beading which glittered in the dim hall light.

"What do you want?" she asked.

"I want to speak to you privately."

"This is as private an interview as you'll get," she said coolly.

The reflection of the hall light on her monocle produced an eerie illusion. It was as though she were glaring at him with one malignant golden eye.

"What do you want?" she repeated. "If it's money, you can't have it. This is not a charitable institution or a home for convicts."

In the pause that followed he made a mental calculation as to the strength of the chain that held him from admission. He might at a pinch break it and force an entrance. He was prepared to go to any mad lengths to get the information he sought.

"Where is my child?" he asked.

Not a muscle of the big face moved.

"I didn't know you'd been raising a family. Surely I'm the last person in the world to be acquainted with your vicarious progeny."

"Where is Jane's child? Perhaps you'll understand that."

She had been taken aback by the first question, he was sure. The length of time that elapsed before she answered betrayed her.

"So you know that, do you? The child? I'm afraid I can't tell you. I have something better to do than to keep track of the indiscretions of my friends, and certainly I do not concern myself with the illegitimate children of convicted forgers—"

"You lie," said Peter quietly. "You know I was married to Jane."

Anita Bellini chuckled.

"The marriage was illegal; didn't you know that? You didn't comply with certain formalities—"

"I have seen Jane to-night. She has no doubt about its legality. Where is my son?"

"Where you will never find him." All the pent-up malignity of the woman suddenly took expression. Her face, never attractive, was contorted by rage to an appearance that was almost ludicrous. "Where you will never find him! In the slime and the mud where his father belongs; dead, I hope!"

A sudden insane fury possessed him. He was scarcely human; saw the hateful face of this woman through a redness, and flung himself against the door. It jerked back with a crash and suddenly flew open. The chain had broken.

To him she was no longer a woman, but some devil that had taken human shape. He wanted to kill her, to grip that big throat and choke the life out of her. As the chain broke, she stepped back, and he found himself looking into the black muzzle of a pistol.

"Don't move," she said gratingly. "Don't move, Peter Dawlish. I am justified in shooting you in the defense of my life."

She did not see his hand move. The pistol was struck down from her grip and fell with a clatter on the floor; and, in his mad anger, with murder in his heart, his hand was outflung. Then somebody called him.

"Peter!"

At the sound of the voice his arm dropped, paralyzed with amazement. A woman was in the hall; she had come out of a room at the foot of the broad stairway; a woman in black silk, white-haired, hard-faced; it was his mother!

"Come in here."

She pointed to the open door of the room and he walked past her without another glance at Anita Bellini. She was shrinking back against the wall, frightened for the first time in her life.

It was a small study furnished in the Oriental fashion; there was a great silken divan, and a shaded lantern hung from the ceiling. Something more modern he saw—a telephone on the tiny octagonal table. The receiver was off—he had interrupted her in the act of telephoning.

"What is the meaning of this?"

Mrs. Dawlish had assumed the old air that he knew so well and detested so much.

He was still shaking, but he was calmer.

"I presume you don't need to be told; you must have heard. I came to your friend—"

"To the Princess Bellini," interrupted the woman. "Yes?"

"To discover where was my child."

"Really?" The gray eyebrows rose. "I was not aware that I was a grandmother."

The old devil rose again in him.

"Then your hearing is affected," he said harshly. "You know—of course you know! The whole gang of you know! You know about Jane, you know about my marriage, you know about the child. Perhaps you know where he is."

And then, to add to the fire of his fury, he saw her smile.

"You have always been a fool, Peter. I suppose you will be a fool to the end of your days," she said. "You had better go back to your envelope addressing and forget there are such things in the world as children. I have been trying very hard to do the same for the past seven years."

She was a surprising woman, for without warning she came back to the offer she had made to him.

"You would be well advised to go to Canada or Australia, or any other place that takes your fancy," she said, and went on in a conversational tone to discuss the advantages which might accrue.

He was puzzled. Then it occurred to him that she was talking to gain time—for what? His back had been to the door and now he edged round until it was under his view. But if Anita Bellini contemplated any treachery, there was no visible or audible evidence.

He heard the front-door bell ring, and an exchange of voices in the hall, and then the door opened and two men entered. It was not necessary that he should be very experienced in such matters to realize that they were detectives. His mother's narrative stopped automatically. Her white, skinny finger pointed to him.

"This man is Peter Dawlish—an ex-convict!" she said. "I charge him with threatening to murder my friend Princess Anita Bellini."

A quarter of an hour after, the taxicab which Peter had employed to bring him to Wimbledon deposited him at the police station, and he was sitting, dazed and wrathful, behind the locked door of a police cell.

CHAPTER XVI.
AN OLD RECORD

"I can't believe it." Leslie stared at the inspector. "His own mother charged him? How monstrous!"

Mr. Coldwell had reached an age where it was almost impossible to surprise him.

"Queer, isn't it? But, Lord bless you, mothers do rum things! I've known cases—but you've heard about 'em, too, Leslie. Peter went down to Wimbledon to raise the devil for some reason or other. It appears his mother had heard the fuss he was making at the door and telephoned for the police before he broke in. It might have been bad for him if he were a convict on license, but fortunately he's time-expired, and he has only to say that it was a family quarrel to get bound over. I don't think he will be called upon for defense, anyway."

Leslie Maughan nibbled at the end of her glove, a devastating habit of hers in moments of perturbation.

"I really can't believe it, though of course it must have happened. What was his mother doing down there? And why on earth did Peter do such a mad thing?"

Coldwell smiled.

"Go down and ask him," he said. "I'll give you a note to the inspector, and you might have a few minutes' talk with him before he appears in court. It is very unlikely that they will remand him to Brixton. If the princess has got horse sense she will get him acquitted. Mrs. Dawlish is pretty sick and sorry that she allowed herself to charge him. I can tell you that because, as soon as I heard about the case, I phoned up the station and the sergeant in charge told me that Mrs. Dawlish came to the police station at seven o'clock this morning to see if she could get her name taken out of the record. She'd allowed her spite to lead her astray, and she knows that when it comes into court, the story of a mother charging her son is going to make a pretty big newspaper sensation. That is why I think that the charge may be withdrawn."

When Leslie reached the police station she found that Peter had been transferred to the cells adjoining the court, and her own card was sufficient to obtain an interview. He met her with a rueful smile.

"You see me again in my natural environment," he said cheerfully.

"Why did you go to Bellini's?"

"I wanted to learn something," he said, and he would not explain any more.

She told him of the inspector's prophecy, but he seemed careless as to whether the charge would be supported.

"It was certainly a facer," he said. "I didn't expect my mother to take that line. I suppose until then I had not realized how bitterly she hated me. They may go on with the charge, knowing that in any circumstances I should not tell what brought me to Wimbledon."

She did not press him for any further particulars. The interview took place in the passage adjoining the court; policemen and prisoners were passing every few seconds, and the conditions were not favourable to confidences. She told him of her own alarming experience, and when she had finished he whistled.

"That explains everything—the chain on the door and old Simms being on guard. I never saw the old devil again after I broke in."

She made no attempt to hide her astonishment.

"I don't see why a chain on Anita Bellini's door explains a little yellow man in my room," she said.

"It does—most emphatically."

Just then his name was called by the court usher and she followed him into court. Peter had hardly been put in the steel pen when the detective sergeant who had arrested him stood up, and addressed the bench.

"This case, your Worship, arose from a visit which the prisoner paid to the house of the Princess Anita Bellini last night. The prisoner, who is a very distant relative of the princess's, had some sort of grievance, and the argument became so heated that Her Highness was compelled to telephone for the police. The princess has no wish to prosecute the prisoner in the circumstances, or to bring a family quarrel into court, and in these circumstances I don't propose to produce any evidence, your worship."

"But the charge is attempted murder," said the presiding magistrate.

"The charge was only taken last night," explained the detective, "and it was the intention of the police to ask for a remand. But the princess has modified her statement, and I am advised that a conviction could not follow on the evidence that she would offer. In those circumstances I ask your worship to discharge Dawlish."

The magistrate nodded, and that was the end of the proceedings. Peter walked out of the dock and joined the girl in front of the police court.

At first he refused her invitation to drive him back to town.

"You're coming with me," she said firmly. "I have a lot of things to say to you and a list of questions as long as Lucretia's grocery order. Probably you will not answer them, but that is beside the point."

They were crossing Putney Common when she leaned over and spoke to the driver, and, slowing down, he brought the car to the edge of the path.

"Let us go for a little walk," she said, and no sooner were they out of earshot than she asked: "Why did you go to Princess Bellini's last night, Peter Dawlish?"

"To find out something."

"What did you want to know?"

Should he tell her? He could not understand himself. Why should he hesitate to take her into his confidence, she who knew so much? And yet he felt an unaccountable shyness. It was as though the confession would make a perceptible difference in their curious friendship. At last he blurted out the truth.

"Jane had a child," he said.

She stopped, and her deep violet eyes met his.

"*Your* child—well?"

He was astonished by the coolness with which she received this momentous news.

"Did you guess?" he asked.

She shook her head.

"I knew," she answered quietly. "It was born at a little farm called Appledore, near Carlisle."

He was momentarily paralyzed.

"You knew—all the time?" he stammered.

"I knew all the time," she repeated. "I knew you had a child, before I knew you were married. It was at Appledore that I found the book of poems, and your little blank verse. And that was why I wasn't quite sure you were married. Naturally she would call herself Mrs. Dawlish in the circumstances."

They were passing a park bench and she caught his arm and drew him down.

"I'll tell you all about it, shall I?" And when she added: "I was spending a holiday in Cumberland, and I suppose it was fate that led me to this very farmhouse. The old lady, Mrs. Still, who owned the place was a widow, and rather a garrulous old soul, but very kind. It was only natural she should tell me of the interesting people who had stayed with her. One of the most interesting was a pretty girl, whose baby was born in the very room I occupied. She came in February, before the season had started—there is a season in Cumberland, you know—and stayed till the beginning of April. She called herself—it doesn't matter what she called herself—but it was not Jane Dawlish. The child was born on the seventeenth of March—St. Patrick's Day. The old lady, who was half Irish, remembered that fact because she had sent a bunch of shamrock up to the pretty lady the morning the child was born."

"Who was with her?" asked Peter huskily.

"Two women—a nurse, and somebody who was obviously Anita Bellini. No doctor was called in; apparently the other woman was a maternity nurse, and it was not necessary to call for medical assistance. My old Appledore lady never saw the baby; she wasn't even sure when it was taken away, but she thought it was on the second day following the birth, because that was the day a man came from London. The 'man' was obviously Druze. She arrived just before Mrs. Still went into Carlisle to do her midweek shopping, and when she returned Druze had gone. The old lady did not know that the baby had gone, too, until the end of the week, when she asked to be allowed to see it and was told that it had been sent off to a warmer climate. The only thing she knew was that it was a boy; the nurse had told her that, and the Appledore lady was rather disappointed because, as she said, the pretty lady had been praying and hoping for a girl.

"Why she should pray or hope for a baby of either sex is a little beyond me, but I have no reason to doubt the truth of the old lady's statement. She showed me very proudly a little book that the 'pretty young thing' was in the habit of reading, a book of poems; and then I saw your ridiculous acrostic. Just about this time I was rather intrigued by certain things which had happened to Lady Raytham. We had, in fact, information at Scotland Yard that she was paying blackmail, and I naturally connected the two events: her appearance here under an assumed name, the birth of the child, and the fact that she was paying out large sums of money from time to time for some unknown service. When, about an hour before I left the farm, old Mrs. Still said that she had heard one of the women speak about 'Peter,' I was pretty sure that I was on the right track."

"Do you know the name of the nurse? Was it Martha—"

"Martha!" She sprang up and stared at him. "Martha? What do you know about Martha?"

He was a little dumfounded by the effect of his words.

"Tell me—tell me quickly," she said impatiently, and he produced from his pocket the letter he had received, and which had brought him to Jane Raytham.

She looked at the pencilled words.

"Martha's servant. That was Druze's sister," she said suddenly. "She had the child. Peter, I am going on this new trail, and you mustn't interfere until I've followed this thing to the end."

"What do you think of me, I wonder?" he asked.

She eyed him steadily.

"What should I think of you? You're unfortunate, Peter Dawlish. I've told you that before."

He shook his head with a wry smile.

"You don't know how fortunate I am," he said, and she laughed in spite of herself.

"Come back to the car, or we'll find ourselves indulging in an orgy of mutual self-pity."

It did not occur to Peter that he should ask her why the self-pity should be mutual, but he never forgot her words.

She dropped him in the centre of London and, going on to Scotland Yard, interviewed her chief and received permission from him to take a day off. Her first step was to get into telephonic communication with the chief detective of Plymouth, who promised to call her up as soon as his inquiries were completed. Though she was on a holiday, there were many official interruptions.

First there came the man who had arrested Mrs. Inglethorne to tell her that that unrepentant lady had been remanded, and to expose the red-faced woman's shocking history. Her maiden name had been Zamosser. She was of Dutch origin, though her parents had lived for many years in England; and with the exception of a very short interval she had been either in the hands or under the observation of the police. She was a receiver, and worse; had been convicted of shoplifting, and, except for one interval in her early youth when she seemed to have lived so respectable a life that the police had no trace of her, she had been in and out of prison since she was a child.

"What about the children?" asked Leslie, anticipating the reply.

The sergeant laughed.

"One of them's hers; the others are what she calls 'adopted.' That is to say, they have been inconvenient children of whom she has taken charge for a small weekly sum or for a larger payment cash down. The only one we have been able to trace is a little boy."

For a moment wild hopes had surged up into Leslie's heart, but they were to die at his words.

"Oh, you've traced the boy?" she said. She remembered the wizened little fellow who had looked up at her with big, sleepy eyes when she had made her incursion to the kitchen.

"Well, we've found his mother, at any rate. The other children mostly belong to poor little working-class girls."

"Are there many baby farmers in England?"

"Thousands," said the officer, and her heart sank. "They're supposed to be under police supervision, but of course they're not. There is no law to prevent anybody adopting a child, though the actual adoption is not recognized in law."

"There is no list of them?"

He shook his head.

"There may be a few hundred on the books. You would know that better yourself, Miss Maughan, as you're at the Yard."

And then, unconsciously extinguishing her last lingering hope:

"I was once asked to trace a little baby that had been handed over to a 'farmer,' but it is like looking for a needle in a haystack, trying to find an 'adopted child' after trace has been lost of it," he said. "A few of them drift into the workhouse schools; most of them die. It doesn't pay the kind of woman who makes a living out of that sort of thing to feed them properly. There should be a State institution where unwanted children could be taken and cared for and become an asset to the country."

He had been gone half an hour when the Plymouth call came through and the news was not especially helpful. Martha Druze had qualified as a maternity nurse in the years '89-'90, and had left the hospital to take up a private position as a general nurse. It was believed she had gone abroad, but there was no actual evidence of this fact except that the present matron, who remembered her, had received a postal card mailed at Port Said a month or two after Martha had gone away. There was also a rumour that she had married very well, to somebody who was variously described as a carpenter of Cape Town and a rancher in Australia. There was only one clue which was faintly promising. Martha was known to have registered herself in the books of a London agency, the name of which Leslie jotted down.

As soon as the conversation was through, she searched the telephone directory for the nurses' agency. It was not there; possibly it had been overwhelmed by competition and had died, as so many other agencies die, from sheer inanition. To make absolutely sure on this point she called up one well-known woman agent and asked her a question.

"Ashley's Agency? Oh, yes. It is now called the Central Nurses' Bureau—in fact, we are Ashley's Agency, though we never use that title!"

Leslie explained who she was and what she required.

"If you'll come round, we will show you the old books; we still have them," was the encouraging reply.

Leslie Maughan put on her hat and coat and went out at once. Halfway down she remembered Mr. Coldwell's gift and went back to buckle on a most uncomfortable garter. The premises of the agency were off Regent Street, no great distance to walk, and she was there in five minutes.

The secretary, who had replied to her telephone message, was already selecting the books for her inspection, and by great good fortune the first of these she had discovered contained the very information that the girl had asked for.

"Yes, we have her on our books—Martha Druze. She applied to us before she left Plymouth Hospital apparently, for that is her original address, and we placed her in a situation in the early part of 1891."

The secretary had opened the book and her finger pointed to a line. Leslie read; she found herself gripping tight to the edge of the table. Looking at her, the secretary saw that her eyes were blazing and wondered what there was in this simple record to engender such excitement.

"It was the only job we ever got for her—" she began.

Leslie shook her head.

"She would not want another," she said.

CHAPTER XVII.
THE TELLTALE PERFUME

When Lady Raytham had begun a letter to her husband the district messenger arrived with Leslie's note. His lordship, in his aimless way, had gone on to Bombay, and was suffering from an old trouble of his; had written a very long letter describing minutely his many symptoms, and had expressed—this was unexpected—the desire that she should go out to him.

She read Leslie's note:

> Dear Jane: Won't you come round and see me? I've got the whole day off, and there is a tremendous lot that I want to talk to you about, not as a poor apology for a policewoman, but as a very human girl who would love to smooth over some of the rough road you are treading. Lucretia has orders to say that I'm out and to admit nobody. I can give you a home-made lunch, and can promise that you will suffer no ill effects therefrom. Or we can lunch regally at or near the Carlton. Please come.

Jane scribbled a note which was delivered to the waiting messenger, locked away her half-finished letter in the bureau, and went up into her room to change. Lucretia had no sooner ushered Jane in to Leslie when she burst out talking.

"Did you see Peter? What happened? I'm so worried about it. I nearly called you up this morning."

"I shouldn't have known," said Leslie. "At least, I should have known he'd been arrested—"

"Arrested?"

This was obviously news to Jane Raytham, for her face went white. Leslie explained what had happened.

"How could she? How could she?" demanded Jane Raytham vehemently. "It was wicked! But how like her! Poor Peter! He lives everlastingly in rough seas."

And then the note of anger in her voice turned to one of anxiety.

"Did Anita tell him anything?"

"Not what he wanted to know," replied Leslie.

The visitor was quick to understand the meaning of that reply.

"Do you know why he went?"

"He went to find his child."

The beautiful face of Jane Raytham flushed a delicate pink, and paled again.

"My child," she said, in a low voice. "I suppose you despise me, don't you?"

Leslie shook her head.

"No, why should I? If I despised every woman who had a baby—"

"I don't mean that. But I allowed them to take it away. I didn't want to, Leslie. Will you believe that? I wanted to keep the child with me. I fought hard for him. The compromise was a desperately weak one, but at least I gained that point."

"What was the compromise?"

Lady Raytham smiled faintly.

"If you didn't despise me before, you'll despise me now," she said.

She was at the fireplace in her old attitude: arm along the mantel, forehead resting on the back of her hand, her eyes fixed on the fire.

"They agreed to that. If it was a girl I should keep her; if it was a boy, he should go away. A mad, wicked idea, so grossly unfair to the child! But I'm terribly tender toward girls. I can't see a girl suffer without experiencing a shrivelled-up feeling inside. I wonder if you know what my girlhood was. If it had been a girl I should have kept her with me and braved everything. But it was a boy—a wonderful boy—they told me of it afterward. I wish I'd seen him, known him, if only for a day, but then I should never, never have allowed him to go."

She turned her face away and her shoulders shook. Leslie sat at the desk and drew fantastic, meaningless arabesques upon her blotting pad; and when that storm of sobbing had died down she said:

"I suppose it is absurd to ask you if there is any clue by which the child could be traced? Of course you've explored every avenue. You've discovered nothing?"

Jane was manipulating her handkerchief, her back toward her, and there was finality in the shake of her head.

"No. I've already tried. I didn't tell Anita, but for months I've had detectives searching. I thought he was in a happy home, you know; I never dreamed that he'd been left."

She could not go on. It was quite a long time before she mastered her emotion.

"Druze told me that night—that horrible night she went away. Laughed in my face when I asked her where the child was. That is why I went after her. I guessed that she had gone to Anita's, and when I found her dead on the path I was frantic. I thought she must have some hidden paper that would tell me. But when I searched, there was nothing—nothing!"

Jane Raytham turned her face away from the girl.

"I have no justification—none," she said. "I was just wickedly selfish. Even if he'd been illegitimate I could not be excused. Illegitimate!" She smiled bitterly. "Thank God I've had no children since I married Raytham! He was not keen about children, or about me for the matter of that. Our married life has been a sort of—modified celibacy!"

She took down a photograph from a mantelshelf and looked at it.

"This is Mr. Coldwell, isn't it?"

Leslie nodded.

"It would be a great feather in his cap if he—arrested me for bigamy."

"Mr. Coldwell is not frantically keen on feathers of that kind, Jane," said the girl loyally.

Jane put down the photograph and dropped into the nearest armchair, curling her legs up under her.

"I'm a beast! I'm putting the worst construction on everything; taking the most uncharitable view of everybody."

She smiled pitifully, reached out her hand for her bag that lay on the table, and snapped open a diamond-encrusted cigarette case.

"I tried drugging once," she said; "a white powder you sniff up your nose. For some reason it made me deathly sick, and I didn't pursue the practice. But I envy people who can find relief and forgetfulness."

"Another good way," said Leslie brutally, "is to put your head on a railway track when a large, fat freight train is due! You'd accomplish the same result, and give much less trouble to other people. And presently, when your boy emerges from the mist, as he will, he would come to a mother who was hardly worth finding."

Jane was laughing quietly.

"You're a weird girl. How old are you?"

Leslie told her.

"I wish Peter was in love with you. He must find happiness somewhere or other."

"Do I come into this?" asked Leslie dryly. "Or are Peter and you the only two people in the world whose feelings count?"

She stopped Jane's penitence with a laughing gesture.

"I'll tell you something, Jane. I'm rather in love with Peter; do you feel faint?"

"I'm not a little bit faint." But Jane was more than a little bit curious. "You're not jesting?"

"I decided this morning that I was very much in love with him," said Leslie calmly, "but I've thought a long time about it, and have reached the conclusion that it is rather my maternal instinct that is operating. I'm loving him in a motherly fashion, in fact. Sooner or later that boy of yours is going to be found, and then you've got to go to your husband and tell him the truth."

She was watching Jane's face closely, ready to note and spring upon the first visible sign of repugnance. But Jane was listening; and listening, the girl realized her heart sinking with approval.

"And then Lord Raytham must give you up, and Peter and you must start afresh."

Here was the first note of dissent. Jane shook her head.

"Peter is different," she said. "I realized it when I saw him last night. He's not the same man. And can you wonder? Leslie, I never loved him. You'll think that's a horrible thing to say of the father of my child. He represented—I don't know, curiosity, I suppose—adventure—the grand hairpin turn of life, where so much is upset and smashed, so many hopes and ideals die. And he never loved me. He was infatuated and he was fond of me, and had a wonderful chivalrous feeling that he was rescuing me from something. That is half his trouble now, that he knows he didn't love me, and it makes him feel ugly and ashamed. You think the child may bring us together. I'm becoming quite a thought reader! But that sort of thing really doesn't happen, does it? Children really do not determine very much. Half the women who are divorced have children who love them and whom they love, but it didn't prevent—things happening. I think Peter and I might be good friends, and the boy might love us both, even though we were apart, for children give you back what you give to them. I could give him such a lot."

With an impatient shake of her head she sat up and walked resolutely to the window.

"Let us talk of rabbits," she said. "How did you break this?" she asked.

For a new and unpainted sash had been put into the window space that morning.

"Never mind about that. A visitor put his head through it. Jane, you're taking rather a hopeless view of life, aren't you?"

The woman shrugged.

"My dear, what can happen? If this were a story and it wasn't real life, I should go away somewhere, contract a malignant fever and die to soft, slow music! But I refuse to offer myself up as a sacrifice in order that my story shall have a smooth and a happy ending! And if I die, Peter will endow me with all sorts of gentle qualities which I don't possess, and will pass the rest of his life in the twilight of melancholy. I know men!"

Leslie was laughing softly. She had too keen a sense of humour not to appreciate the fact that this entanglement had its funny side. Suddenly she became serious.

"There are only a few questions I want to ask you, that I've never asked before. Did you give Druze your emerald necklace?"

Jane nodded.

"Yes. This mythical person wanted thirty thousand pounds. I could only draw twenty without Raytham knowing. The necklace was worth twelve thousand, and I suggested that Druze should sell it. She jumped at the chance. I thought she had taken it away a week before she actually did."

"You can't account for the pendant being found in her hand?"

Jane shook her head.

"And you don't know where the rest of the chain is to be found?"

"I am absolutely ignorant. I can't conceive how she met her death. It is only reasonable to suppose that she had a life and friends of whom I knew nothing. Where she went, after she left my house, I do not know. I guessed she was going to Anita's because she would not leave England without saying good-bye: she was very much attached to Anita."

"How long after your baby was born were you married to Lord Raytham?"

Jane considered.

"About ten months," she said.

"Did you go to Reno personally?"

"Yes," Jane said. "That was one of the queer coincidences of it all. My father had a small farm near Reno, just a shack and a few acres of ground, and this was accepted as a residential qualification. Of course, I had to lie desperately and say I was living there all the time, and really I believed the divorce would go through. I even appeared in court and gave my evidence, and I thought that the thing was settled, until Anita saw me outside the court-house and told me that my lawyers had made a bungle and that the divorce could not be granted without serving some papers upon Peter. I went straight away with her; her automobile was waiting, for I was scared of the reporters, who were all the time hunting marriage romances for their newspapers. Besides, the baby was coming. I was frightened that people would know."

"And you returned immediately?"

Jane nodded.

"Yes; I went to Cumberland from Liverpool. Anita discovered the place. It was some time after Christmas; I remember that I was in New York on Christmas Day."

"There is one final question, Jane, and then I'll stop being a mark of interrogation and take you out to lunch. That is, if you don't mind being seen in public with a Scotland Yard female?"

"If you wish," said Jane, with the first spark of animation she had shown, "I will eat my lunch out of a paper bag with you, seated on top of one of Landseer's lions!"

"This is the question," said Leslie, slowly and deliberately. "Marriage with Lord Raytham was in the air, wasn't it, and you had discussed it with Anita?"

Jane nodded.

"And did she know of your intention of marrying Raytham whether the divorce was granted or not? Please think very carefully before you answer."

"There's no need to think very carefully. I told Anita that I should marry Raytham whether the divorce was granted or not. I salved my conscience by expressing doubt as to the validity of the marriage."

Leslie leaned back in her chair with a large and happy smile.

"You're a wicked conspirator, a perfectly horrible mother, and not a tremendous success in any of your matrimonial ventures!" She slipped her arm round the woman's waist and kissed her on the cheek. "But you're rather a darling. We'll lunch at the Pall Mall, which is terribly nice for women, and we'll occupy the afternoon with a movie. I love the movies—especially the romantic ones!"

She was rather relieved than otherwise when, nearing the end of luncheon, Jane remembered, with some contrition, that she had promised to be at home that afternoon to receive a committee of which she was chairman.

"Child welfare," she said laconically. "The angels weep every time I sit at the head of that board and dilate upon the duty of mothers! Raytham, in spite of queer little ways, is a dear where these societies are concerned, and he's fearfully in earnest about them. I drew the line when he wanted me to take control of a committee which helps fallen women. That was stretching my sense of humour to a breaking point."

They parted in the Haymarket, and Leslie went back to her flat, stopping on her way to wire to Peter. He came when the day was fading and Lucretia was drawing the curtains. Two stout suitcases were ready packed in the hall, and during the afternoon Coldwell had called her up with strict injunction to be ready for him when he came.

"I'm not going to allow you to stay in the flat until this little business is finished," he said.

Here he had a strong supporter in Lucretia Brown.

"Not for a million pounds would I stay in this place after dark, miss," she said. "What with burglars and people jumping out of the window and what not, I wonder I've got any hair left! When I combed it this morning it came out in handfuls."

"The remedy for that is shingling," suggested Leslie, and Lucretia grew sardonic.

"When I want to look like a boy I'll wear trousers, miss!" she said. "Not that I've anything to say against shingling, which suits you very well, because you've got the kind of head. And as for these bingles with your ears sticking out all over the place like the Princess Bellorino or whatever her name is—I call that disgusting! The only use for ears is to hear with, not to go pushing theirselves out into the world, so to speak. I was hoping her ladyship was coming back this afternoon, miss. A bit of society does nobody any harm."

"If she'd only known, I'm sure she'd have jumped at the opportunity of giving us a social lift," said Leslie, and Lucretia sniffed. She was not very thin-skinned, but she always knew when her young lady was indulging in what Lucretia described as "sarc."

"I only want to say—" she began.

"There's the bell," interrupted Leslie. "If it is Mr. Dawlish, shoot him up."

"A low convict!" murmured Lucretia, but she murmured it under her breath.

The convict was neither lowly nor humble. Leslie had never seen him look more serious, and the old flippancy of his tone was gone. It was a very determined young man who sat down at the opposite side of her writing table.

He had been making inquiries, he said.

"It is a hopeless business when you don't know where to start. I thought Jane would give me a hint, but of course the poor girl is as much in the dark as I. Yes, I am awfully sorry for her. I'm afraid I was rather a brute."

"She doesn't think you were," said Leslie lightly.

"Have you seen her?" he asked quickly.

"This morning," she nodded. "In fact, I lunched with her. We talked over the whole grisly affair from A to Z. Are you very much in love with her?"

He shook his head.

"I'm not in love with her at all. I suppose I ought to be, right down in the deeps of my heart, but I'm not. And she is not in love with me, either. I knew that seven years ago. She was not over-reticent when she came to discuss our marriage before the separation. Did she tell you anything at all about the boy?"

"Nothing. She really doesn't know."

He agreed.

"I was sure she didn't. Bellini knows—no, I won't call her princess or Anita or anything feminine or human! She's just a devil—a wicked devil! How my father hated her! I've an idea he was a bit afraid of her, too. I remember once he asked me, when we were walking together at our place in Hertfordshire, if I liked her, and when I told him that the sight of her made me ill, he put his hand in his pocket and gave me a golden sovereign! And yet he must have been very fond of her once."

"Fond of her?" Leslie's eyebrows met. "Do you seriously mean that?"

"I do. They say she was awfully attractive—not very pretty but very attractive—when she was younger."

Leslie pushed back her chair.

"This has been a most educational day!" she said. "Produce your evidence, Mr. Dawlish, that your father was ever attracted by that monstrous lady."

He tried to turn the conversation, but she kept him to it remorselessly.

"I shouldn't have known, only my mother and the princess quarrelled. I was curled up in a chair in the library—I must have been about seven—reading one of the kind of books that my father used to buy for me—about pirates and cutthroats and the usual exemplar of youth—when they came into the library together. My mother was furious with Bellini. I didn't understand all it signified at the time, but later, when I came to think it over, it seemed pretty plain. My mother was furious. 'You've had your inning,' she said. 'He doesn't like you any more, and he doesn't want you in the house. You won't get him back, anyway.' There was a lot more said on both sides that I cannot remember. I know that it ended in my mother crying and going out of the room, and in Anita Bellini leaving the house. They must have been on bad terms for two years, probably three. Time has no meaning to a child."

Leslie was chewing the end of a pen-holder.

"Then your father, in the argot of these days, was a bad lad?" she said.

"I wouldn't say that," he protested. "He was a very simple man, attracted by clever women; and Bellini was brilliant. I remember that her husband was alive in those days—a very tall, thin, melancholy Italian who spoke very bad English. My father and he were not very good friends. I think Bellini had borrowed money and hadn't repaid it, and dear old Donald Dawlish was rather a stickler for commercial honesty."

And then, with a half-ashamed laugh:

"I don't know why I should be slandering my father or gossiping when I should have no other thought than of my boy. Did she tell you whether she named it?"

"It was neither named nor registered," was Leslie's reply. "From that point of view the child has no existence, and that is why he is going to be so very difficult to trace."

The pen quivered between her white teeth; she stared out of the window.

"I wonder—" she said softly.

"What do you wonder?"

"If the other two pieces in this jig-saw puzzle are going to be so easy to fit. And I wonder other things, Peter Dawlish. Where is the screw I can turn on Anita Bellini? Give me that letter you had."

He took it from his pocket and she read it.

"Who sent you this?"

"There was no name attached."

She looked at the envelope and the postmark.

"This was sent by one who wishes to do either Jane or the princess a pretty bad turn," she said. "Now if I could only trace the sender—"

She lifted the letter to her nose and sniffed daintily.

"A clever detective would be able to tell in an instant if this perfume was chenel No. 6 or chypre. I, being an ignoramus, only know that Greta Gurden's bedroom reeked with it!"

CHAPTER XVIII.
ANITA'S FRIGHT

At that moment Greta Gurden's bedroom reeked with the pungent scent of frying sausages that wafted in from the little gas-ring in her "dining hall." When Greta was her own provider, she was economical to the point of stinginess. She, who would hesitate languidly between sole Mariner and sole à la bonne femme, who chose the most delicate and expensive of ices, and who had a pretty knowledge of the virtues of relative vintages, when she had an escort to foot the bill, could find, in the intimacy of her flat, the ingredients of complete satisfaction hanging from a hook at the local butcher's.

She had been allowed to get up that afternoon and found that she could drag herself from room to room without pain or inconvenience. Mrs. Hobbs had gone home, having a husband of her own to serve, and Greta was left alone, and was glad.

Face-saving is a practice which is not wholly Chinese. When she prepared her mean little snacks she liked to be by herself, for she was one of those who desire to be thought well of by the least accountable of people. She was almost cheerful as she speared the sausages from their sizzling bed and laid them on a hot plate, brewed the tea from a kettle placed before the gas stove, and, spreading a cloth across half the table, prepared to enjoy her evening repast.

She had not heard from Anita since the woman's visit, and she had spent the greater part of the day regretting the spirit of malice which had induced her to send an eight-year-old sheet of paper to Peter Dawlish. Fortunately, Anita would never know; that was the one solace she had. What would Anita say if she discovered? Greta shuddered to think.

Being malicious, she was a coward; and it was cowardice which brought about a revulsion of feeling toward the employer she betrayed. In the processes of reaction, she felt almost tenderly toward the victim of her spite. Nevertheless, the finding of the letter had given Greta an idea. There might be other documents equally valuable, remembering that the day was near at hand when her sole legitimate source of income would perish in the inevitable liquidation of *Mayfair Gossip*.

It was all very well for Anita to sneer and rail at the paper, but it had been a very good friend of hers. There were two prominent announcements printed week after week in the pages of this scurrilous little organ; the first of these was called "Stories of Real Life," and it was announced that for the sender of the best material from which such a story could be constructed there was a weekly reward of twenty-five pounds. Stress was laid upon one point, that the material must be authentic, that it must be spicy, and that it must be remarkable. The second announcement was to the effect that contributors who were in a position to secure social items of interest would be well paid.

These two appeals produced a voluminous correspondence, the majority of which was valueless for their purpose; but sometimes an aggrieved servant would reveal matters that were even outside the cognizance of her employer. The maid who found a bundle of old love letters in a secret drawer of her master's desk was very well rewarded indeed. Those letters went on to Anita, who found an excellent use for them.

Officially, Greta knew nothing of these matters. Officially, she was sending on these letters because they had a piquant interest for her employer. She was never asked to do anything that a lady could not do, or even that Greta could not do. She made a very good use of the smaller and less important items that reached the office, for Greta was an efficient, if one-sided, journalist. She had one formula which she followed in every case.

> Dear Anita: The inclosed letters are not, I am afraid, of much use
> to the paper. We shall be prosecuted for libel if we dare use one
> tenth of what is in them. They may, however, interest you.

The letter never varied; it had become almost a stereotype.

She contributed special articles to *Gossip* and because of a sojourn of four-teen days in the United States had become an authority upon the Four Hundred, could talk glibly and inaccurately of the leaders of society, and occasionally would introduce a Long Island colour to her paragraphs. She could write fairly well, had a mordant wit of her own, and in happier circumstances might have become a great journalist. Instead of which she had developed insensibly into a cringing sycophant, dependent upon a wage that was paid in all the circumstances of charity.

As she ate her three large, indigestible sausages, she decided to tackle that night the last bundle of letters which needed reading and classifying. It was therefore not an inappropriate moment for Anita to call. Mrs. Gurden stood up like a soldier when the woman swung into the room and pulled the door close behind her.

"Your leg's all right, is it? Good! I want you to come over to Wimbledon to-night."

"My dear Anita, I couldn't possibly come to-night," broke in Mrs. Gurden, a picture of sweetness and delight at seeing this unwelcome visitor. "The doctor says—"

"I don't care what the doctor says," replied Anita brusquely. "You've got to come over to May Towers."

Greta murmured something half-heartedly, and made a final fight.

"It may be fatal," she said in a hushed voice. "The doctor—"

Princess Bellini said something very uncomplimentary about doctors in general, and glanced at the remnants of the humble meal with a sneer which she did not attempt to conceal.

"Pack all your things, everything you want for a long stay," she said. "I'll send one of my people up to help you if you like, but it would be better if your own woman—Snobbs or Hobbs or whatever you call her—helped you."

"How long do you want me to stay?" asked Greta in consternation. She counted the most unhappy days and nights of her life those she had spent as Anita's guest.

"A month; six weeks possibly—I'm not sure," said the woman brusquely. "I'm going to pay you very well indeed. As for your leg, I've telephoned to your doctor and he tells me that you're fit to move, and in fact the wound is healed."

"But the paper—"

"The paper is dead. I've written to the printers telling them so. My lawyer will liquidate the business, so that's off your mind. You've got to do something, Greta. Your source of income from that direction has dried up."

Greta listened in dismay, and offered the weak comment that it "seemed a pity." And then, with a resolution which was born of her very feebleness, she said:

"I can't go. I simply won't go, Anita, until I've seen the doctor. You're most inconsiderate! I haven't recovered. It isn't only the wound, it's the shock of—Druze's death. I simply won't risk my life. After all, I have to take care of myself. Gurden doesn't care a darn whether I'm alive or dead."

Anita sat squarely before her, her big hands on her knees, her eyeglass fixed in her impassive face.

"Gurden!" she rasped. "You almost make this ghost of yours real! You've got to the end of your argument, Greta, when you call on the precious name of Gurden. He belongs to the same order as Mrs. 'Arris."

"It's not true, it's not true!" protested the haggard woman tearfully. "We're married but we're separated."

Nevertheless, she proceeded to give no further details that would elucidate that mystery of her life.

"Whether you are or whether you're not, you're to come over to May Towers," said the princess definitely. "If you want to see a doctor, you can send for any one you like."

Greta elected for her own doctor, but he was out and not expected back until late that night. She ran her fingers down the directory of the profession, seeking a familiar name, and presently she found one and rang him up. Anita, renovating her toilet before the looking glass in the bedroom, heard Greta speaking in her sugary society voice, and smiled grimly.

"If you please, Doctor. I wondered if you would remember me. It's most awfully kind of you—no, only a little scratch. The wound has quite healed, I'm sure, but I should like to see you ever so much."

There was a click as the receiver was hung up. Anita smoothed the powder on her face, gave her large, shapeless lips a touch of a red, creamy stick, and strolled back to the dining room.

"Well, have you found your doctor?"

"Yes, Anita, I have," said the other. "He's a very nice man and he won't let me go out if he thinks that it's dangerous to my health. And really, I must consider myself, Anita, sometimes. I'm not at all well, and I've been thinking for a long time of placing myself in a doctor's hands—"

"Whom have you sent for?"

"Doctor Elford Wesley. He used to be old Mr. Dawlish's doctor—"

She heard a growl like the sound of a beast and stared aghast at Anita. Her eyes were wide open; she showed her teeth in an ugly grin.

"You brainless fool!" she exclaimed. "Why did you send for him?"

CHAPTER XIX.
CAPTURED

Demoniacal, terrifying, she towered above the frightened woman, and Greta cowered and held up her hand as though to ward off a blow.

"Get on the telephone, quick, and tell him he needn't come. Invent any excuse you like! Hurry!"

In a trembling voice Greta called the number.

"He's gone," she said, and looked up at her mistress.

"All right, hang up, you fool!" Anita was breathing quickly. New lines showed in her face; she looked like an old woman.

"Send somebody down to the door and tell him he needn't come."

"But, Anita," wailed the other, "I can't do that! I must see him, Nita. What a stupid thing you are! What difference does it make? If you don't like him you needn't show yourself. And if I send down a message like that he'll be awfully suspicious! You remember how the police came just because my wretched doctor told somebody I had a gunshot wound in the leg?"

There was reason and intelligence in this, and though the woman was quivering between fear and fury, she had no course but to assent, and when, ten minutes later, the doctor's foot sounded on the stairs outside, Anita Bellini disappeared into the bedroom, but did not go beyond earshot.

He was an elderly man, rather talkative and fussy, short and stout, with a cherubic face and short white side whiskers.

"Bless my soul, I remember you now!" he said. He was one of the loud and jovial race of doctors that is fast dying out. "I remember you very well. You used to be a friend of the Dawlishes, didn't you? Poor old Donald! What a good sort! Now let me look at this leg of yours."

He examined the wound, which was little more than a scar, and, to Greta's dismay, pronounced her fit to travel.

"You'll have to take care of yourself for a week or two," he said conventionally, and returned to the topic his examination had interrupted. "Yes. I was with old Donald two days before he died, from morning till night, hoping against hope that I could do something for him. For twenty-four hours I never stirred from his side. Poor old Donald! He died six hours after I left him, with my dear friend, Sir Paul Grayley, one of the best doctors that ever lived."

Old Dr. Wesley was blessed with this disposition, that all the people he knew were the best people that ever lived, and all who were bereft of his acquaintance came under the generic heading of "poor souls."

"Very bad business about his boy, poor soul!" He shook his hoary head. "Terribly bad business. I didn't know Peter personally—never met him. But when I heard of this fearful thing he'd done, I said to myself, 'My boy, if the news has to be broken to Donald you're the man to do it.'"

He was very talkative, very delightful, very human, but Greta was annoyed with him and gave him little encouragement to stay. As for the woman standing in the darkness of the bedroom, had her wishes materialized, old Doctor Wesley would have been swept from the face of the earth.

Presently he was gone, and she came out from her listening post.

"Apparently you can move without dying," she said sarcastically.

"Apparently I can, if I want to move." Greta's voice was husky. She was back in her last trench, conscious of a great shortage of ammunition. "And I don't want to move, and that's flat! I can't understand why you hate that dear old man. I admit he's fearfully chatty, but that's no reason why you should throw a fit at the mention of his name."

"When I want your opinion about my peculiarities I will ask you for it," bullied Anita, and it was a wrong move, as she realized.

Mrs. Gurden shrugged her shoulders rapidly.

"If that's the tone you're going to adopt," she said, with an heroic assumption of boldness, "the sooner we part the better, Anita. You've stopped the paper, but I think I'm entitled to some money instead of notice; and if it comes to that, I've had no salary for a month. And as to going down to your beastly old Towers, I simply won't, so there!"

The princess forced a smile.

"My dear Greta, you're getting theatrical. But I realize you're not quite yourself. Now don't be a little fool. Come and rest with me for a week or two. There are one or two big schemes I want to talk over with you, and afterward we'll pack up and go to Capri or Monte Carlo or somewhere's a little more cheerful than Wimbledon."

"I won't!"

It required a tremendous amount of courage to utter those two words of defiance, but it was zero hour to Greta Gurden, and for the moment she had all the ferocity of a mad sheep.

"I simply won't! If I've got to earn my own living, I'll earn it. I can get a job on *Fleet Fashions*. I was offered one last week. I'm tired of your domination and your bullying, and—well, I simply won't go to Wimbledon, and that's a fact!"

Here was a resistance which Anita Bellini had never anticipated. There was not the stuff of sweet reasonableness in her. She had made her way in the world by the force of her character, and her simulations had been confined to hiding her too-frequent fits of anger. It was not in her to persuade; she must command or do nothing.

"You're going to make me look foolish. I've promised—"

"I don't care what I make you look." Greta's head was quivering with determination. "It's not my fault. And whom have you promised?"

Without waiting for a reply, she said:

"You know how I loathe that house at Wimbledon and those awfully creepy Japanese men of yours."

"Javanese. They're quite nice people. If you refer to your encyclopædia you will discover they are inoffensive, peace loving, and domestic."

But sarcasm was wasted on Greta.

"That may be or may not be," she said. "All I know is that I'm not coming with you."

"Stay and be—stay till to-morrow!" exclaimed the elder woman. "I shan't waste my time or go down on my hands and knees to you. You owe me a lot, Greta—"

"You owe me a month's salary," said the spirited Greta, with admirable courage, "and three months' notice."

Her hands trembling with rage, Anita tore open her bag and flung a packet of one-pound notes on the table. Without another word she strode out of the room and shut the door so violently that the whole house shook.

Greta Gurden sat bolt upright, shivering with triumph, yet with a sinking sense of terror at what the morrow would bring forth. She had charred her boats but she had not burned them. Her shaking hand grabbed the telephone.

"Put me on to Scotland Yard," she said.

She heard the weary sigh of the operator.

"Is Scotland Yard blessed with a number?" she asked.

Greta hung up the phone and looked round in search of the directory. But apparently Scotland Yard had no number, nor did there seem to be such a

place on the face of the earth. She was to learn later that the official designation was New Scotland Yard, but she did not dream of looking under the
"N's." And then she remembered Leslie Maughan, and the "M's" yielded a
good result. She waited for a while after she had given the number, and then:

"Yes. I want to speak to you."

"Yes, Mrs. Gurden."

Greta started.

"How did you know?"

She heard a laugh.

"I always remember voices, especially nice voices like yours," said the men-
dacious young lady from Scotland Yard.

"I want to see you very much—very badly, I mean—tremendously."

"In fact, you want to see me," said Leslie. "I'll come along."

It required some persuasion to induce Lucretia to wait for the arrival of Mr.
Coldwell.

"Very well, then," said Leslie patiently. "Wait in the street. You'll catch your
death of cold, but I don't suppose that will worry you very much. You might
even hobnob with a policeman. I trust you."

"I should jolly well say you did!" said the indignant Lucretia.

She compromised by sitting on the baggage in the passage, the door being
propped open with a weight. She found it a little more drafty than the street.

Greta's boats seemed a little more burned than she could have desired
when she surveyed the desolation just before Leslie's arrival. She had little stamina for quarrelling, and already her mind was a confusion of fear
and penitence when Mrs. Hobbs, who had returned for her evening duties,
showed the girl into the dining room.

"It's awfully good of you to come." Greta was her conventional self; grabbed
the girl's hand in both of hers; used that old and artless trick of looking up
pleadingly into her visitor's face. "I'm so worried, my dear. The truth is, I've
quarrelled with Anita. Definitely and finally," she said, recovering a little of
her lost ground. "The paper is dead, as you've probably heard—you know
everything at Scotland Yard. That means I'm out of a job, though I can get
one to-morrow by asking. Anita has behaved abominably. I should never have
dreamed, after all I've been to her, the thought and care and experience I have
devoted to her, as it were— Do take your hat and coat off. Shall I ask the maid
to make you a cup of tea?"

Leslie, secretly amused, shook her head. She guessed that the woman had
changed her mind since she first sent for her. It was hardly likely that she
would trouble to telephone about one of those quarrels which, if her informa-

tion was accurate, were not an infrequent occurrence between Greta Gurden and the princess.

"Of course, I've nothing to tell you that would harm Anita." Mrs. Gurden planted one foot firmly on shore, and prepared, figuratively, to splash the waves of her venom with the other. "But she's so peculiar—and such a temper! I shouldn't be surprised if she goes off in a fit of apoplexy one of these days."

"What is her trouble now?"

Greta could tell her this much, she decided, without disloyalty to her late employer. The very thought that she was "late" filled her with dismay.

"She wanted me to go to Wimbledon to stay there for a month, and I hate the place, I simply loathe it! I'm rather temperamental; I suppose all artists are—I mean artists and literary people. And May Towers gives me the horrors. And, of course, she was terribly rude to me, in spite of the fact that I am far from well and my leg aches excruciatingly. Anita is the most unreasonable person. You've no idea, Miss Maughan. Of course we quarrelled, and I simply told her that I'd have no more to do with her. And then she made a fearful scene because I asked old Doctor Wesley to come up and see me and tell me whether I was fit to be moved. She practically cursed me for calling him. Really, I thought she was going mad. And he's such a dear old soul—awfully talkative, of course, but a perfect gentleman, and a kind man."

Leslie was sitting at the other side of the table, her hands folded patiently, waiting for the real story to come. Now she leaned forward, her eyes upon the woman's face.

"Doctor Wesley? Was he the Dawlishes' doctor?"

"A very charming old man but awfully fond of Mr. Dawlish. Except for six hours just before his death, he was with old Mr. Dawlish for a whole day and a night—never left his side."

Leslie hardly heard the next five minutes' complaint, but when she came to bring her understanding to bear upon her hostess, Greta was not much nearer to the reason for her telephone message.

"If anything comes out I can always say, and Anita must bear me out, that I never knew this wretched man was a woman. The first thing I saw was Anita and this man struggling, and I wanted to send for the police. And then those wretched men came in and tried to drag the pistol out of Druze's hand—her hand, I mean. And there was I, lying on a sofa—fainted, my dear, and with simply not a notion in the world that I was wounded. It may sound strange to you, but it is true. When I woke up, Anita was going on like somebody who had lost her head. It was simply ghastly."

"Did you see Druze again?"

Greta shook her head.

"No—the language she used before the shooting started!" Greta shuddered. "I simply couldn't repeat half the words she employed. Of course, Anita sent me out of the room; said she didn't know I was there; but just as I started to go out, my dear—bang!" Mrs. Gurden grew dramatic and illustrative. "Bang! And then everything went dark. You know how it does, my dear."

"I can't understand quite," said Leslie. "A few hours after the shooting I found you at Lady Raytham's."

"She sent me—Anita," Mrs. Gurden broke in. " 'Go to Jane, but tell her nothing,' said Anita. 'Find out all that you can about Druze—how they parted, if she threatened her.' Those were her words. You know Anita—she's—what is the word? Imperious! I didn't know whether I was on my head or my heels—like that Mr. What's-his-name who's written a story about women. I simply had to! And not an idea in my head that a beastly bullet had gone into my leg. The doctor said that if I hadn't run about the wound would have healed right away. It was only when I got home, my dear, I nearly died!"

She paused to take breath.

"I suppose she'll come to-morrow and ask me to go back. I'm such a forgiving nature."

"If there is anything in life that you value, you will stay here, Mrs. Gurden," said Leslie quietly. "I don't want to frighten you, but I think it is my duty to warn you that the Princess Bellini's course is nearly run. As to Druze—"

She had never thought that Druze was murdered; always she had had at the back of her mind the possibility of a struggle in which the shots were accidentally fired. There was a good and sufficient reason why Anita Bellini should not shoot the mock butler.

When she reached her flat, the front door was closed. She opened it and turned on the passage light. Lucretia and the grips were gone, she saw with satisfaction. In the letter box was a blue-lettered cablegram and she snatched it out and opened it. This was a reply to one she had sent on her way back from lunch, and she read the message and could have sung in her joy.

She ran up the stairs, her mind divided between this blessed message and her interview with Greta Gurden. Greta was in revolt; that much was clear. But how far would her rage and venom carry her toward a complete betrayal of her employer? As she passed the hall window, she noticed that the new safety catch was in place. Really it was ridiculous to leave the flat at all, she thought. After that one attempt it was not likely that a second would be made.

She almost regretted now that she had agreed to Mr. Coldwell's plan. Throwing open the door of her sitting room, she put out her hand and turned the light switch. But the room remained in darkness. Had they replaced the fuses? she wondered, and walked into the room.

There was no sound, no warning. A great hand suddenly gripped her throat, another covered her mouth. She felt the pressure of a knee in her back and struggled desperately but unavailingly.

"You scream—you killed!" whispered a voice in her ear, and, summoning all her strength, she tried to nod in agreement with the unspoken demand of her captor.

The door closed softly behind her. There were two men. She felt her ankles gripped and lifted, and she was carried into the bedroom and laid on the bed.

"You scream—you killed!" said the voice again.

The grip about her throat relaxed, but the evil-smelling hand was still on her face.

"I won't scream," she managed to mumble, and the stifling palm was removed.

"You scream, I cut your t'roat. You not scream, I not cut your t'roat—not hurt."

"I shan't scream," she said in a low voice. "May I get up, please?"

There was a whispered consultation in a language which held some gutturals, and then the man who had first spoken said:

"You sit on a chair, keep very quiet, long time, long time."

He gripped her by the arm and assisted her back to the dining room, guiding her to a chair, though there was enough light from a street lamp for her to pick her way.

There were two men—little men; their heads were not much above her shoulder. Broad, squat, and, as she had reason to know, immensely strong. She could not see their faces; by accident or arrangement their backs were to the window. He who was evidently chief of the two said something in an unknown language, and his companion withdrew to the landing, and the hall and landing lights went out. Presently he came back, and, to her surprise, he was joined by a third. Again there was a whispered consultation, and the third man disappeared, the other two squatting on the carpet before her, impassive, silent, watching, as she guessed, with eyes that did not leave her for a second. A quarter of an hour they sat thus, and then:

"I speak English liddle bit. I hear English well," said the man. "I tell you trut'. Last night you get t'roat cut. This night no hurt." He added a phrase she could not understand.

"What are you going to do with me?" she asked.

"Presently by and by," said the little man, after he had repeated her words slowly and had grasped their meaning, "you and me walk into car. While you walk you see peoples. If you speak to peoples I cut your t'roat."

Very definite, but the repetition of the phrase amused her mildly.

"You're rather monotonous, aren't you?" she asked. "And after I get into the car what happens?"

There was a pause while he took this in.

"By and by you see," he said.

The third man came back now, and she gathered that he was in reality the leading member of the gang, for on his word the two others vanished through the door and he took their place.

"You won't be hurt unless you give us trouble," he said. To her surprise he spoke in perfect English. "My patron requires you."

"Who is your patron?"

It gave her a sense of comfort to know that this queer little shape could understand all she said, and could converse intelligently. It made him less of a strange and menacing animal, and removed some of the terror from the situation. And it delayed the moment when she would find her cumbersome garter a vital safeguard.

"I cannot answer your questions, miss," he replied. "But you will not be hurt. Last night you would have been killed—I myself would have killed you—but that is not the order to-day. If you are sensible and quiet, nothing will happen."

He stood up and looked out of the window; neither the shades nor the curtains had been drawn, and he could see to the opposite side of the road.

"I must tell you what will occur," he said. He had a trick of pedantry which might have amused her at any other time. "This house is being watched by the police. After a while they will grow tired and careless, and then my friend will signal to me that they have walked away. When that happens we will go."

She could not see him; she could only guess that his "friend" was one of the two. She had noticed that all three were dressed in correct European garb, and the incongruity of their overcoats and derby hats added a touch of the bizarre.

"Will you therefore sit nearer to the window, at your writing place? If the telephone rings you will not answer."

So they sat, he on one side of the table and she on the other, his eyes roving to the sidewalk, and from the sidewalk to his prisoner. She saw the limousines stream past on their way to the theatres, and wondered if, on any stage in

London, there would be enacted a drama quite as improbable as this in which she played a leading part.

After a long interval of silence:

"I suppose you realize that, when I do not arrive at Mr. Coldwell's house, he will either telephone or come back for me?"

He nodded.

"We have already made provision," he said simply. "We have sent him a telegram in your name, saying that you have been called away to"—he hesitated—"I cannot remember the town; it is in the west and is on the sea."

"Plymouth?" she asked quickly.

"Plymouth," he said. "The telegram also told him your hotel. Plymouth is very far, and by the time he discovers you have not arrived"—a pause—"by that time you will not be here."

"Where shall I be?" she asked.

But the only answer was a strange, solemn glance.

CHAPTER XX.
A SILK SHAWL

Children—little Elizabeth and that unseen boy of his! Peter Dawlish walked up and down his cramped room, his hands in his pockets, an unlighted cigarette between his lips. The hopelessness of it all! Where and how could he begin his search? That baby of his belonged to the world of unreality, to the mists of dreams. Elizabeth was real. He could see those wide, frightened eyes of hers, the transparent pallor of her face. He shut his eyes and there she was again, frail, delicate, pleading for help he was powerless to give.

He was alone in the house. Through the thin partition walls which separated one jerry-built cottage from the other he heard the sound of a man and a wife quarrelling. In the street a boy was whistling flatly a popular tune. If Mrs. Inglethorne were here he would have the truth though he had to choke it from her. Who else would know but she?

He had been such a short time in the lodging that he was not even acquainted with her friends; the slinking little thieves who came to barter and haggle over the property they had stolen knew no more of her than that she was a mean and grinding bargainer. She had no cronies to come and spend the evening with her; by very reason of her peculiar business, she could not risk the giving or taking of confidences.

The police had been to the house and made a perfunctory search, their object being to discover other evidence against her. But they had looked only for articles of value which she might have purchased; lengths of cloth and silk—she specialized in this trade—and they were not particularly concerned about Elizabeth. Nobody cared very much about Elizabeth, except Leslie and he.

This thought occurred to him as he walked to and fro—and thought breeds thought. Might he not, searching with another object, discover what they had overlooked—one fragment of a clue that would bring him to the child? Why should he be concerned? What legal or moral right had he to detach Mrs.

Inglethorne's daughter from her legal guardian? He considered this matter, only to brush it aside. Presently he carried the lamp downstairs, with the faintly pleasurable hope which comes to all who engage in secret searches.

The woman's room was accessible. The lock he had broken had not been repaired. He went in, put the lamp on the mantelpiece and looked around. Search parties usually leave chaos behind them, but the police in their investigation had, if anything, tidied the room. There were a number of dresses, obviously the woman's, stacked on the bed. Two oleographs that once decorated the wall had been lifted down—clean squares on the wall paper marked their old position. By the side of the clothes was a square wooden box, of the kind that soldiers use for the transportation of their possessions. This had been opened and was unlocked. The lid had jammed upon a wedge of cloth as it had been closed, and there was a gap of an inch.

Where would a woman like Mrs. Inglethorne keep papers? Or did she keep papers at all? He tried to remember the habits of her type, acquired at second hand from his fortuitous acquaintances in Dartmoor Prison. Under her bed? But the police had obviously rolled up the mattress and made that elementary examination. There was nothing here—nothing. He opened the big black box, disparagingly. And then he saw, with a quickening interest, that the inside of the lid was almost covered by newspaper cuttings which had been pasted on the wood. Here was revealed Mrs. Inglethorne's "scrap-book," and incidentally her favourite daydream. A headline caught his eye.

HEIRESS TRACED BY HER BABY SOCK

Another headline ran:

CHILD'S MOTHER TRACKED BY INITIAL ON INFANT'S GOWN

He carried the lamp to a little table and read the cuttings carefully. They all dealt with one subject: The identification of unknown children that had brought fabulous fortunes to the lucky person who had traced their descent. Some of the cuttings were very old, yellow with age, and scarcely decipherable. Evidently Mrs. Inglethorne's collection covered a long period.

He supposed the police had searched the box, which was nearly filled with little cylinder-shaped bundles tied around with tape. Linen, coarse calico, cotton—diving into the mass, his fingers touched silk. The bundles had once been white, but constant fingering and dust had left them an indescribable hue. He untied a bundle and opened it. It consisted of a child's cotton night-dress, a little pair of woollen shoes, and a small knitted shawl. Pinned to the shoes was a scrap of paper on which was written in an illiterate hand the words: "Mrs. Larse, boy, ten days old, measles, nine months." Here then was the beginning and end of Mrs. Larse's boy. "Measles, nine months" was his epitaph.

She was a baby farmer; he had guessed that. He opened another bundle hopefully. Somewhere here would be a reference to Elizabeth. The second package had nothing but a coarse calico robe and a penned inscription: "Young girl named Leavey, five days, whooping cough, six weeks." One by one he unrolled these little tragedies, and few indeed were they who had not their death certificates inscribed laconically at the end. Some had two papers, identically inscribed. He supposed that the repetition was due to Mrs. Inglethorne's careless and haphazard system of "bookkeeping."

He had examined twelve and took out the thirteenth, wondering what potency there was in that lucky or unlucky number. The nightdress he unrolled was of the finest linen, the most expensive of all he had examined. The shawl was of heavy silk, and the microscopic shirt of the most delicate flannel. For some time he could not find the inscription, but eventually it was discovered inside the shawl. Only three words, but they set his heart beating.

"Miss Martha's girl."

The bundle dropped from his nerveless hands. "Miss Martha's girl!"

He took the letter out of his pocket. "I have found a home for your son and—" He read again the pencilled words "Martha's servant." And Martha's servant was—Mrs. Inglethorne!

Miss Martha's girl. This woman could not have made a mistake. One by one he examined the clothes separately, and then, pinned to the inside of the dress, near the collar, he found a second paper written in the same hand, and, reading it, he uttered a hoarse cry.

"Miss Martha's girl Elizabeth."

Feverishly he untied the other bundles but found no further clue. His knees were trembling as he mounted the stairs, the precious garments close to his heart. Putting down the lamp on the table, he examined again these pitiful souvenirs. He must see Leslie at once. Not daring to leave the clothes behind, he folded them and put them into his pocket. He used the silk shawl as a neckcloth under his thin overcoat; the night was bitterly cold, but it was not the warmth of the soft fabric which brought a glow to his heart.

The windows of the flat were in darkness, but he remembered that they had heavy velvet curtains, and possibly they were drawn. Ringing the bell, he waited. There was no answer. He rang again. And then a man appeared from a near-by doorway and strolled up to him.

"Who do you want?" he asked, in a tone of authority. Peter guessed that he was a detective.

"I want Miss Maughan. My name is Dawlish."

"Oh, Dawlish, yes. Miss Maughan isn't in. She is staying at Inspector Coldwell's house in Finchley. There is nobody in the flat."

He did not hide his disappointment; he was so full of his discovery that he had to tell somebody. He had to see her. The detective gave him the inspector's address and he walked across the Charing Cross Road, intending to make his way to the tube station. He reached the other side of the road, and then something made him look back at the windows of her apartments. And in that instant he saw a quick flicker of light, as though somebody had turned on an electric hand lamp for the fraction of a second and had extinguished it immediately.

Peter stopped. Somebody was in Leslie's room. He walked slowly across the road. The detective had disappeared; was, in point of fact, walking to the back of the block to visit his fellow watcher. As Peter stood, hesitating, he saw the street door move slightly, and, acting on an impulse, he pushed it wide open and took one step into the darkness.

"Who's there?" he said, and that was all that he remembered.

Something soft and heavy fell with a thud on his head, crushing his soft hat as though it were paper. He stumbled on to his knees, and a second blow laid him prostrate, the blood trickling down his face and staining the soft silk that had once enwrapped his child.

There were no loiterers in Charing Cross Road that bitter night, when a chill northwest wind sent people hurrying to the shelter of their homes. There was no lounger to tell the detective of three people who had walked hurriedly across the sidewalk into the car which was drawing to the curb at the very moment Peter pushed open the door.

CHAPTER XXI.
ANITA'S CARDS

As the car moved off a man came running across the road, stepped lightly on to the foot-board and wriggled his way to a place beside the driver. The car was held up outside the Hippodrome but only for a few seconds, and then, turning, it sped wheezily along Coventry Street. They had a good crossing of Piccadilly Circus, and a few seconds later they had struck the gloom of lower Piccadilly and had turned into Hyde Park.

Leslie had a glimpse now of the faces of her captors: yellow, with that Oriental slant of the eye which is common to the Chinese and Japanese. Here the likeness ended; their faces lacked the intelligence of the people of the island kingdoms.

Javanese, of course! How stupid she had been not to have realized that from the first! Anita Bellini had lived in Java for many years. And then she remembered Peter's words. She understood the chained door because of the attack that had been made on her flat. Anita's bodyguard had been engaged elsewhere; she had need of chains to protect her house in their absence.

The car slipped across Hammersmith Bridge, and after a few minutes she could identify the spot where the body of Druze had been found. They were going to Wimbledon, then—to Anita's grisly house.

The machine came to a stop before the door of May Towers and she hurried up the steps. She had not reached the top before the door was opened. No light showed in the hall, and she heard the door clang behind her and a chain rattle as it was fastened, and her courage almost deserted her. Somebody flashed the light of a hand lamp; she saw the wide, heavily carpeted stairs.

"Go up," said her conductor, his hand still on her arm, and she obeyed.

The stairs turned and they reached a wide landing. Somebody knocked at a door, and a voice which she recognized as Anita's said:

"Come in."

The man who had knocked pushed the door open wide. She had a glimpse of a lofty wall, hidden by a black curtain which was covered with curious designs in gold threadwork. The room was filled with an unearthly greenish light; the hand of the jailer fell from her arm; she walked into the room alone, and the door closed behind her.

It was a long and ill-proportioned salon. With the exception of a divan at the far end and a low table near by, it was bare of furniture. The carpet underfoot was either purple or black; in the queer light of two green lamps that burned on either side of the settee it was impossible to distinguish its colour.

Anita Bellini sat cross-legged on the divan, horribly suggestive of some repellent and grotesque idol in her golden frock. Her massive arms were smothered from wrist to elbow with glittering bracelets. Three ropes of pearls hung about her strong neck, and every time her hands moved they sparkled and scintillated brilliantly. A long ebony cigarette holder was between her lips; that immovable monocle of hers gleamed greenly.

"Come along, Maughan; sit here." She pointed to the floor, and, black against black, invisible from where she had paused when she had entered the room, Leslie saw a heap of cushions.

She sat obediently, looking up into the coarse face. So they sat surveying one another for a space, and then, flicking the ash from her cigarette, Anita Bellini spoke.

"You have brains, I suppose?"

"I suppose so," said Leslie coolly.

"Sufficient brains to know that I wouldn't take the risk of bringing you here—abducting is the word, I think—unless my position was rather desperate. I'd have killed you last night, but that would have been a fatal mistake. You are much more useful to me alive."

Leslie smiled faintly.

"Which sounds like a line from a melodrama!" she said.

"The Javanese are a gentle, kindly people," Anita said slowly, "but in some ways—they are not nice."

"I understand this is a threat as to what will happen to me if I do not do something you wish?"

"You're a sensible girl," said Anita Bellini, and leaned forward, her elbows on her knees. She was very much like a fishwife in that attitude; there was something inexpressibly common about her, in spite of her monocle and her Parisian gown, and the luxury of her surroundings. "This afternoon"—she was still speaking very slowly and distinctly—"Coldwell applied to the Bow

Street magistrate for a warrant—a warrant for my arrest and a search of this house. Did you know that?"

Leslie was genuinely astonished and shook her head.

"I had no idea, and I can't think that what you say is true," she said. "Mr. Coldwell made no mention of any such arrest; in fact, I was spending the night at his house, and I know he had arranged—"

Anita broke into her explanation.

"He applied. Whether the warrant was granted or not, I do not know. That is one point. Another is this: you visited Greta Gurden to-night, and she told you the one thing in the world I wished that she should not tell—I know because I saw you go in and come out of her flat, and I have seen Greta since," she added grimly. "It isn't necessary for me to tell you the vital information you discovered."

"It isn't," said Leslie. "But I might have found that out anyway. In fact, I should, if I'd had the sense to go straight to Doctor Wesley and ask him how long before Donald Dawlish's death he was unconscious. I've always suspected that the alteration of that will was a forgery. I saw a copy of it, and I have compared it with the signature of Donald Dawlish. It would not have been very difficult to prove that the new will which gave Mrs. Dawlish the whole of her husband's fortune and which disinherited Peter, was a forgery from beginning to end. The doctor will, of course, prove that beyond any question. On the day he was supposed to have made the new will, Mr. Dawlish did not recover consciousness. Surely, Princess, you don't imagine that you will get away with that! Mr. Dawlish's lawyers have always been dissatisfied with the will that was made without consultation, and which was only proved because they could not induce Peter Dawlish to contest its validity."

Anita Bellini made no answer to this.

"I'm chiefly concerned with myself and my own safety," she said at last. "You've got to help me, and Martha must look after herself. You've got to help clear me. I'm going to make you a very good offer—a hundred thousand pounds."

Leslie shook her head.

"Not all the money in the world will influence me, Princess," she said. "How could I clear you? You talk as though I were the chief of the Detective Bureau and had authority to divert the processes of the law! The person you must see is Lady Raytham, whom you have blackmailed for years, and even if she were agreeable, the law requires that you shall explain the death of Annie Druze."

"It was an accident."

Leslie nodded.

"I know—or rather, I guessed. But that has got to come into the light, and it cannot come into the light unless the story of the blackmail is revealed. I am willing to do this: let me walk out of your door unharmed, and the little adventure of to-night will be forgotten. I will forget your Javanese, I will forget what happened last night. Tell me where I can find"—she paused—"Elizabeth Dawlish."

"There is no such person," said Anita harshly.

"Elizabeth Dawlish," repeated Leslie, "Peter's daughter."

Princess Anita Bellini was not smoking now. She had the holder in her hand, turning it over and over and examining it critically as though she were looking for some defect.

"You've got to get me out of this mess, Leslie Maughan."

Leslie rose to her feet.

"I thought you were clever!" she said, with a note of contempt in her voice. "Nothing can get you out—nothing!"

"Is that so?" Anita's voice was soft and silky. "Do you realize, my good woman, that if I can't get out, who has put me in—you! You've been prying into the history of the Druzes, have you? Ah, ha!" She laughed harshly. "I know a great deal more than you imagine. And you've been putting the little pieces together to trap Anita—poor old Anita, eh?" She showed her big white teeth in a mirthless smile, and suddenly slipped from the divan and drew near to the girl. She clapped her hands twice.

The room was seemingly empty; yet at that signal half a dozen little men appeared as if by magic from behind the long curtains. Anita, her face swollen with rage, spluttered something and the squat shapes came shuffling toward her.

Leslie did not move. She stood erect, her hands by her sides, her pale face turned to the woman. Even when they seized her, she did not resist, but allowed herself to be hurried behind the fold of a curtain and through a door into a stuffy little room into which she was thrust. The door was closed on her, a lock snapped; from the other side of the door a mocking voice called to her.

"Now I will be avenged."

Leslie stooped, pulled up her skirt, and unstrapped an appendage from a garter. It was a small-calibre weapon. She slipped back the jacket, forced in a cartridge, and brought the catch to safety. Then she began to explore.

The furniture of the room was a little tawdry. The divan, which seemed an indispensable adjunct to every room, was old and worn; a shaded light hung from the ceiling; there were two brass dishes attached to the wall. It appeared to be the apartment of a highly favoured upper servant, and this she confirmed when she turned over the coverings of the divan and saw what was apparently a suit of native clothing.

There was a second door to the room and this she tried. Then, to her surprise and delight, she saw that there was a key on the outside. She turned this, and to her relief it opened, and she found herself in a very conventional bedroom, the type of apartment she would have expected to discover in any of the houses on Wimbledon Common. No lights were burning and it was inadvisable to switch them on. Softly she closed the door of the room she had left, and tiptoeing across the floor, felt her way to the bedroom door. She turned the handle softly and looked out.

Happily, the two men who stood on the landing had their backs turned to her. She closed the door again, in an agony of fear lest she should make a sound. Running quickly across the bedroom, she tried the windows. They were not only fastened and barred, but, as a further barrier to egress, the bars were covered with a stout wire screen. Perhaps there was a bathroom, she thought, and groped along the wall. After a while she felt the handle of a door and opened it gingerly. She must risk putting on the light for a second, and this she did.

It was evidently used as a dressing room, and there was another door which, she guessed, led to a second bedroom. She turned out the lights; the door was locked, and again the key was on the outside. For a moment she suspected a trap and hesitated, but after a moment turned the key and entered the room, only to draw back instantly. Somebody was there; she heard the sound of breathing, and a tiny creak as though a body was turning in bed. And then:

"Who is it, please?" asked a voice, and Leslie nearly dropped.

For the child who spoke from the darkness was Elizabeth!

"Don't make a sound," she whispered, and, taking out the key, closed the door and locked it on the inside.

Only then did she feel for the light switch. The room was a small one and apparently there was no other way out than that by which she had come. The small window was barred and wired; the window itself was of opaque glass. She looked round at Elizabeth; she was sitting up in a small bed, looking with astonishment at this unexpected vision. Then suddenly she leaped out of bed and came running toward the girl, and Leslie caught her in her arms.

"Are you going to take me away? I'm so frightened. These little men frighten me. I told you about them. One came and left the pistol with Mother. Oh, take me away, please, please!"

Leslie gathered the frail form in her arms and kissed her.

"There's nothing to be afraid of," she said, but without any great conviction. "Tell me quickly, Elizabeth! Is there another way out of this room?"

To her surprise, the child pointed to a plain wardrobe which stood against the wall.

"She comes through there sometimes," she whispered. "A terrible woman—with an eyeglass. She told me that if I made any trouble, one of the black men would kill me." The child shuddered.

Putting her gently away, Leslie went to the wardrobe and pulled open the door. The wardrobe was empty and reached from the floor to the height of her head. The back was undoubtedly a door; there was no disguise about it. There was neither keyhole nor handle. Using all her strength, she pushed, and the door swung open; it had been fastened by a very simple spring catch.

She returned to Elizabeth and wrapped a bedspread round her thin shoulders.

"You're to be very brave and very quiet," she whispered. "Come with me."

The child hesitated.

"She told me I must never go through there," she began, but Leslie reassured her, and they passed through into an apartment which was also a bedroom though apparently out of use. The bed was not made, and some of the furniture was shrouded in Holland covers.

Again Leslie opened the main door, this time to find herself on another landing. There was nobody in sight. Down below, at the foot of a narrow flight of stairs, a light burned dimly.

"You've got a pistol, too," whispered the child in wonder, and Leslie smiled.

"Don't talk," she whispered into Elizabeth's ear, and led the way down the stairs.

They terminated in a small passage, paved with tiles. As she reached the foot of the stairs she heard the sound of voices, and, looking round cautiously, she saw that under the stairs was a door, and it was open. At the far end of the passage was another, and this obviously led to the outside of the house, for it was chained and bolted.

As she stood, debating what she should do, the voices grew fainter, and the patch of light on the wall which marked the open door disappeared. It was her chance. Grasping the child by the arm, she slipped off her shoes and hurried noiselessly along the passage in her stockinged feet.

She had reached the door, and with fingers which, in spite of her will, trembled, moved first one chain and then another. The top and bottom bolts were drawn; her hand was on the key, when from somewhere above came an outcry. A bell rang, a door under the stairs was flung open and three men ran out. The first two did not see her, but made for the stairs. The third caught sight of her over his shoulder and yelled a warning. In an instant the three men were flying toward her. Twice the little pistol banged, and one man slid to the ground with a yell, grasping his knee. And then they were on her and she was fighting desperately for life.

She heard the scream of the child and called out to her to open the door and escape. But Elizabeth was too petrified with terror to make any movement.

They carried Leslie Maughan, trussed and bound, into the purple salon and laid her at Anita's feet. And then the man who spoke English lifted his hand.

"Lady," he said, "here is the woman. What shall be done?"

Anita pointed to him with her thick jewelled finger.

"This night you shall have the privilege of torturing her," she said, in her grating voice.

CHAPTER XXII.
A REAL FATHER

It seemed to Peter Dawlish that he had been unconscious for an eternity when he turned over on his back with a groan and carefully felt his damaged head. His face was wet and sticky, and when he essayed to rise to his feet, it seemed that the whole of the building was oscillating violently. Presently, however, he was up, keeping to the wall for support, and, grasping the handle of the door, he jerked it open and was instantly gripped with hands of steel.

"Hullo, who are you?" asked a stern voice.

"I don't know—Dawlish—something happened. I saw a light and came over—and then the door opened and I don't remember much more."

The detective recognized him.

"The door opened?" he said anxiously. "Was somebody in the flat?"

Peter nodded and winced.

"Give me a drink," he said, and the detective guided him by the arm and led him upstairs to Leslie's room.

A glass of ice-cold water revived him and he was able to tell a coherent story of his experience.

"It couldn't have been more than ten minutes ago," said the detective. "I went round to see my opposite number and I'll swear I wasn't gone for more than that time."

Suddenly he stooped to the floor and took up something. It was a loose native slipper that had slipped from the foot of Leslie's captor in the hurry of departure. The light he had shown when he searched for this was the light that Peter saw.

"Just wait! I'll call Mr. Coldwell."

Inspector Coldwell was at dinner when the message came.

"Hang on, I'll come down," he said. "I've had a wire from Miss Maughan that she's going to Plymouth, but that doesn't mean anything."

He was in the flat twenty minutes later. By this time Peter's wound had been roughly dressed, and he had washed the stains from his face. Save for the throb of the wound, he was little the worse for his experience.

"They coshed you with a rubber club; it is rather a good method," said Coldwell callously.

He looked round the room with pursed lips and a frown.

"It doesn't follow that because those birds were here, she was here," he said, and glanced at his watch. "Too early for Miss Maughan to have arrived at Plymouth. Just wait! I want to make sure."

He drove to the telegraph office from which the message had been sent, and was fortunate to find the postmaster just leaving his office.

"I want to see the telegram that was sent from here about five o'clock to-night addressed to me."

"You want to see the original telegram, I suppose? That won't be difficult."

It was more difficult than he supposed, and half an hour's precious time was wasted before the pencilled form was produced. Coldwell had only to glance at the writing to know that it was not in Leslie's hand. Yet a woman had written it; that was obvious from the characteristic writing.

He returned to the flat and sent the detective in a cab to Scotland Yard and Peter employed this interval to tell him of what he had found in Mrs. Inglethorne's box.

"I pretty well guess that," said Inspector Coldwell. "So did Leslie—Miss Maughan. 'The son' meant nothing. This unfortunate lady had intended to keep the child with her if it was a girl, and that was not the wish of the gang who were bleeding her. They told her she had a son. But I'm going to make sure about that before we go any further. Somehow I'm not so scared about Leslie Maughan as I ought to be perhaps. She's got a sort of gun."

A quarter of an hour later, his cab drew up before the gloomy doors of Holloway Prison and after a strict scrutiny of his credentials he was admitted and conducted to one of the main halls of the jail, where the remand prisoners were housed. The chief wardress opened the door and went in. Presently she came out and beckoned him into the cell.

Mrs. Inglethorne was sitting, a scowl on her face, her big, raw hands clasped before her. She knew Coldwell, and lifted her lip in a grin of rage.

"Don't you come in here!" she said shrilly. "I'm not going to talk to you. If you want to find that kid, you go and find her! And that'll take you some time, I'll bet!"

"Listen!" Coldwell had a very direct way with criminals. "Whether you'll get a nine-month or more depends on the answer you give me, Mrs. Inglethorne. There's just a chance that you may get something worse."

She scowled up at him.

"What do you mean?"

Very deliberately he sketched a portion of her life: told her where she had lived, and how long she had stayed in her various places of abode. She made no comment or correction, looking down at her hands, and only when he paused did she meet his eyes.

"Is that all?" she asked insolently.

"Not quite all. You have been engaged in baby farming for the past twenty years. In 1916, in the month of July, you received from one called Arthur Druze a baby boy of a few days old. Where is that child?"

"You'd better find out," she said.

The detective's eyes narrowed.

"It is for you to find out," he said, in that hard, metallic voice which he adopted on occasions. "You have to prove to me that that child is alive or there's another charge against you."

"Eh?" She was startled. The big mouth trembled. "You can't charge me—"

"I'll charge you with murder, and I'll dig up the garden of every house you've occupied in the past six years to find evidence."

Mrs. Inglethorne's many-chinned jaw dropped; her eyes stared wildly, and in their depths Coldwell read the very terror of death.

"I've done nothing—like that!" She almost screamed.

"You were Martha's servant, weren't you?"

She nodded dumbly, and then, throwing herself on the couch, she writhed like a woman demented. And in her dementia she broke the habit of a lifetime and told the truth.

———◦———

A policeman was standing outside the door of Leslie's flat when Coldwell came back, and a dozen men stood about on the sidewalk. He beckoned Peter to him.

"You had better come along," he said.

"Where are you going?"

"To Wimbledon. Do you feel fit enough? There may not be a scrap, but I rather imagine that her supreme and exalted highness will die fighting."

"Is Leslie there?"

Coldwell nodded.

A hundred yards short of May Towers the policemen stopped and the little army of men got down. On the journey Coldwell had made his arrangements. Four of the detectives were to make their way to the back of the house; the remainder were to force the entrance. It was Coldwell who rang the bell. In his right hand he gripped an ax, ready to strike at the chain the moment the door was opened.

Standing behind him, Peter saw him stoop his head.

"Can you hear anything?" he whispered.

"No, sir."

"Thought I heard a scream."

He waited a few seconds longer, and then:

"Give me the crowbar."

Somebody passed him up the long steel bar, and with a swing he drove the clawed ends between door and lintel. Again he struck, and this time he succeeded. Pulling back with all his strength, the door cracked open. Two blows from the ax broke the chain, and they streamed into the dark hall and up the stairs.

The squat Javanese stooped and lifted the girl without an effort, and as he did so the little men who stood around clapped their hands rhythmically. Leslie heard and set her teeth, as she felt herself raised in the strong hands of this hideous little man.

She had a glimpse of Anita Bellini. The hate in her eyes made her shudder in spite of herself.

"Good-bye, little Maughan!" she mocked. "You are going to your death."

And then she stopped, her eyes glaring toward the door.

"Stand fast, everybody! Tell these fellows not to move, Bellini!"

It was Coldwell's voice. Leslie felt herself slipping from the encircling arms. Then, suddenly, somebody caught her, and she looked round into the haggard face of Peter Dawlish.

"No gun play," said Coldwell gently, "and there will be no trouble. I want you, Bellini! I suppose you are prepared for that?"

"I am called Princess Bellini," she said.

"Whether you're Princess Bellini or Annie Druze or Alice Druze is a matter of supreme indifference to me," said Coldwell, as he caught her wrist. "But you have the distinction of being the first woman I've ever handcuffed." He snapped the cold circle about her wrist. "But then, you see, most of the ladies I've pinched have been gentle little souls compared to you."

She made no reply. That old look had come into her face again which Leslie had seen before.

Then Anita Bellini did an unexpectedly generous thing. She nodded to the wondering group of natives, shepherded behind three armed detectives.

"These men have done no harm," she said. "They have merely carried out my instructions in ignorance of the law."

She said something in Javanese to the man who had held Leslie, and he grinned and answered in the same language.

"My head boy here"—she nodded to him—"will accept responsibility for the other natives."

And then, with a sidewise jerk of her head and a hard smile, she said:

"Well, here is the very end of the Druzes."

"Not quite." Leslie's quiet voice interrupted her. "Martha has still to be disposed of."

There was anger, but there was fear also in Anita Bellini's grimace.

"Martha? What do you mean—Martha?" she asked sharply. "I have not seen her for years."

Leslie smiled.

"I saw her two days ago, so I have the advantage of you," she said.

They waited only long enough for Leslie to gather a change of dress and a coat for the prisoner, and thereafter Anita Bellini went out of her life forever, except for the day when Leslie stood in the witness box and testified against the monocled prisoner, who did not look at her but sat staring straight ahead at the scarlet-robed judge.

Before she collected the clothes, she went in search of Elizabeth, and found her weeping in her bed in the little dressing room, and persuaded her to dress. By the time the princess was out of the house and on her way to Wimbledon police station, the child was arrayed in her rags. Leslie stood in the doorway looking at her, and she was very near to tears.

"Elizabeth, do you remember how you used to pretend you had all sorts of nice fathers?"

The child nodded and smiled.

"Well, I'm going to introduce you to a real one."

"A real father?" asked the girl breathlessly. "My father?"

"And you'll never guess who he is."

Suddenly the child was clinging to her, her arms locked about her neck. Thus Peter found them, weeping together.

CHAPTER XXIII.
AND A MOTHER

It was not often that Mrs. Donald Dawlish made a call at any hour of the day. The appearance in Berkeley Square of her big car at eleven o'clock at night was something of an event.

"Mrs. Dawlish?" said Jane in wonder, when the footman came to her with the news. She had not seen the woman for two years. Indeed, Mrs. Dawlish's attitude of late had been frankly antagonistic. "Ask her to come up, please."

The woman strode into the room, patting her mop of untidy white hair into place. She wore the black which suited her better than any more vivid shade, and on her bosom blazed a diamond star which was just a little too large to be altogether ornamental.

"I suppose you're surprised at my coming at this hour?" She dropped her shawl on the settee, and, walking to the fire, held out her hands to the blaze.

"I am a little," said Jane, wondering what was coming next. Nothing short of a catastrophe could have brought Peter's mother in such circumstances.

"I've been a good friend of yours, Jane, in the past," she began, and her look asked for confirmation; but Jane was silent. "There's trouble, bad trouble, over that will of the old man's," she went on. "I've had a letter from his lawyer to-night, asking me to give them all sorts of information that I am not prepared to give. The will was proved six weeks ago. They can do nothing now, but they nag and nag and I'm getting tired of it all. They may be acting for Peter, but I doubt it. But Peter can stop this persecution."

It was the first news that Jane Raytham had had of any trouble in connection with the will, but the request was one which she could not pass unchallenged.

"I know nothing about the matter," she said. "Peter of course must do as he wishes. I have no influence there."

"You have a big influence," said Mrs. Dawlish emphatically. "Peter has found out about the child: I suppose you know that?"

Jane nodded.

"The man is crazy to find it, and he—"

She met the gray eyes and stopped.

"I am crazy to find it, too," said Jane Raytham in a low voice.

"Are you?" Mrs. Dawlish was honestly surprised. "I didn't think you were that kind—to worry about—things. Well, that's all the better from my point of view. I can give you the child. You can tell Peter that I'll give you the child and make him a handsome allowance if he will stop his lawyers from worrying me."

"You can give me the child? You know where he is?" Jane's voice shook.

"Well—yes, I do. It wasn't a boy, Jane."

Jane Raytham shrank back as if she had been struck.

"Not a boy? A girl? And you promised me—"

"There's no sense in talking about promises, or what happened eight years ago," said Margaret Dawlish coldly, "I'm talking about the present. Yes, it was a girl. Druze took her to an old servant of mine—Martha's servant!"

Jane could only stare at her, speechless with amazement.

"You—you're Martha?"

Mrs. Dawlish nodded.

"Martha Druze?"

"Martha Dawlish. I am entitled to that name; not even Peter can take it from me. I married old Dawlish a fortnight after his wife died in childbirth. Anita bullied him into it, if you want to know the truth. She would have married him herself, but Bellini was alive. I was her favourite sister and she always wanted me to make a good marriage. I don't know what she had been to my husband and I don't very much care, but she was an attractive woman in those days, before she let herself go; at any rate she had enough influence to make him marry me."

Jane passed her hands before her eyes, as though she were trying to sweep away the mist which still obscured a clear view.

"You're Martha?" she said again. "Of course, I knew you were a nurse. Then Peter—"

"No, Peter isn't my son, if that is what you're going to say. I insisted that he shouldn't be told. I felt it would weaken my position and authority. Mr. Dawlish was rather an easy-going man and he agreed. If Peter had had the brains of a gnat he wouldn't have needed telling. He had only to see the registration of his birth and compare it with my marriage certificate to know as much as you know now. Jane, will you help me with him? I don't care how large the allowance I make him is—"

Jane shook her head helplessly.

"I don't know what I can do. I can't think very clearly, only—I want the child—my girl."

The hard face of Mrs. Dawlish creased in a rare smile.

"Is there nobody else who wants her?" she asked significantly. "Has Peter no rights? You haven't thought of that, I suppose?"

"I have thought of it," said Jane in a low voice. "But I know Peter. And whether I or he have her, she will be free to us both. We're going very swiftly down the slope, and the slope is getting steeper and Heaven knows where we shall land at the bottom. I've been just as wicked as a woman can be. I'm a bigamist—don't interrupt me, please—I'm a bigamist and my husband must know. I don't think it will worry him as much as it worries me, and in a way he'll be rather glad to get rid of me. But I can face all that if I have my baby! I'll do what I can," she went on quickly, recovering the lost balance, "if it doesn't hurt Peter. I've hurt him enough. He is too good a man to be wounded any further. I cannot see him to-night; I will write to him and ask if I may see him to-morrow, and then—"

The door was opening slowly and a man came in whose head was bandaged. At first she did not recognize him, and then:

"Why—why, Peter!" she faltered.

He was leading by the hand a little girl in a worn, stained ulster. The golden head was hatless. Jane Raytham looked down into that beautiful child face, saw the clear eyes looking at her wonderingly, solemnly, and put up her hand to her throat, hardly daring to speak. She opened her lips; no sound came. She made yet another effort.

"Who is this, Peter?"

It was not like her own voice.

"This is Elizabeth," said Peter gently. "Elizabeth"—he stooped and looked into the child's face—"Elizabeth, this is your mother!"

CHAPTER XXIV.
THESE WOMEN

"I'm sorry to have brought you down to this very unpretentious little flat of mine," said Leslie, "but I have discovered in myself some of the qualities of a showman, and really and truly, most of the documents and proofs I have are here."

And then she laughed, rocking from side to side in her chair.

"What is the joke?" asked Coldwell suspiciously.

"You look so like Christy minstrels, all sitting round in a circle with your hands on your knees, and it's three o'clock in the morning, and—there are a dozen reasons why I should laugh. I'll begin at the beginning; shall I?

"I suppose everybody knows how I worked up an interest in this case, through finding a book of poems in a little Cumberland farmhouse, and how I put two and several together, made them four, guessed them six, and finally proved their real quantity beyond doubt.

"There was a family living in Devonshire named Druze."

Briefly she retailed all that the clergyman had told her, and all she had learned from subsequent inquiries.

"Annie Druze was in reality Anita. Alice was Arthur Druze, and Martha, the younger of the two, eventually became Mrs. Dawlish. The three girls were very staunch friends. They had made some sort of compact in their childhood to stand together through thick and thin and that is the only creditable aspect of their subsequent careers. Annie went abroad as a lady's maid, and scraped an acquaintance in some way with an impecunious scion of an Italian family and married him. Martha had a training in a hospital, became a maternity nurse, and was subsequently called in to nurse Peter's mother with her first child.

"Alice, the middle sister, joined her sister in Java, where the prince had taken some minor position. I have had a long talk with Martha, and she tells me that Alice Druze became Arthur Druze as the result of a masquerade. She went one night to a fancy-dress ball dressed as a man, and nobody guessed her identity. The possibility may have occurred to Anita, as she had become, that in this guise her sister would be of use to her, for there is little question that even so long ago Anita was engaged in blackmail.

"There is proof that she blackmailed a government official of Java, and there is the record of a complaint made to the English police in '89 when she returned to this country, from the wife of one of her victims. And she did not stop at blackmail. Martha—who, to save her own skin, has betrayed everybody—says that she had forged three bills of exchange to her knowledge. It is established that it was Anita who forged Lord Everreed's signature, and, taking advantage of Peter being out of the way, got Druze to cash the check, the proceeds of which were divided between the two sisters. Whether she did this out of sheer wickedness and with Martha's knowledge in order to ruin Peter, or whether she was in low water, I cannot discover. Martha suggests the latter reason and swears that she knew nothing about the forgery until later. I have my own opinion.

"Anita was distantly acquainted with Jane before Peter knew her, but she did not become interested in her until after her marriage and return to England. The arrest of Peter coincided with Anita's learning that Lord Raytham, a very rich man, was anxious to marry Jane, who in some mysterious fashion had disappeared. Anita guessed the cause and went in search of and found her. She learned of Jane's condition and kept by her, her object being to persuade her to marry Raytham, so that she might profitably exploit the new Lady Raytham. She tried to persuade Jane that her marriage wasn't legal, hoping that the girl in her desperation would commit bigamy and be under her thumb for the rest of her life. But Jane made one desperate attempt to free herself from the marriage. She went to Reno, applied for a divorce, and that divorce was granted."

"Granted?" Jane's voice was shrill, almost a scream. "It was not granted, Leslie; it was refused!"

"It was granted. Your decree was made absolute. I have a cablegram from the clerk of the court to that effect; it arrived last night. Naturally, Anita did her best to prevent the divorce, because, if it were given, she had practically no hold except the child, which was subsequently taken away by her sister and handed to Mrs. Inglethorne, who for four years was in Martha's employment. When she found she couldn't stop the divorce, she induced Jane to go out of court while the judge was giving his decision. Her car was waiting at the door of the court, and Jane was sitting in it, waiting for the verdict. It was not until Anita came out of court and joined her in the car that Jane learned that the divorce had been refused. She married Raytham, believing that she was a bigamist, and yet finding poor sort of comfort in the belief that there had been some sort of irregularity in her marriage which made it invalid.

"For seven years Jane Raytham has been paying toll to the blackmailer, supposedly the man who had charge of the child, in reality to Anita Bellini and her sister.

"Immediately after her return from America, Jane went to Appledore, her time being very near at hand. It was then that Martha was called in, and the poor girl learned that her white-aproned nurse was the terrible Mrs. Dawlish whom Peter hated and feared. This was the beginning of Jane's time of torment which endured until a week ago. Then Druze, as I will call her, got scared. I think I was the person responsible. My inquiries about the twenty thousand pounds that had been drawn from Jane's bank, information which came to Scotland Yard in quite a normal way, frightened her and she decided to go abroad, getting as much money as she possibly could before she left.

"Jane gave her her emerald chain, and with this Druze went off to interview her sister. There was some little quarrel as to the division of the spoils. Anita, who was the stronger of the two, snatched the chain from her sister's hands, never expecting that the woman, infuriated with drink and anger, carried a pistol. In the struggle which followed, Druze was shot, but in some miraculous fashion still retained her hold of the square emerald. I can only imagine that Anita was so beside herself with grief that she did not make a search. In a panic she had the body put in the car and taken to the lonely spot and left there. But new clues were coming to light every day. Mrs. Inglethorne reported the presence of Peter Dawlish in her house and his interest in the child. Imagining that he suspected who Elizabeth was, and that his coming to Severall Street was designed, she had the little girl taken to Wimbledon, and concentrated all her mind upon getting rid of my unworthy self. For in me she thought she saw her chief enemy, and I think she was right.

"And that," said Leslie simply, "is that!"

Mr. Coldwell got up stiffly and stretched himself.

"I'm going home to bed. It's very unlikely that you will be troubled by the little yellow boys, and I think I can leave you and your Lucretia here without any misgivings. I don't know how this is going to look in court, or who will be brought into the case and who will not, but those things are the little unpleasantnesses which you will have to live through and live down."

Jane knew he was addressing her and smiled.

"I can live everything down," she said, "and live through everything, if somebody will let that little yellow head sleep on my pillow now and again."

She walked across to Peter and held out her hand.

"I don't know whether I'm glad about the divorce," she said. "I think I am. And I hope you are, Peter."

She cast a swift sidelong glance toward Leslie, who was arranging her papers at the desk, and dropped her voice still lower.

"Do you think somebody else is glad?" she asked.

"I hope so," said Peter, and for the first and last time Jane Raytham felt a little twinge that had a remote resemblance to jealousy.

It was gone in a second.

"Come and see me to-morrow; I want to arrange things for—our family."

And when his lips twitched, she said:

"That smile was almost paternal."

They were all gone at last except Peter and Leslie, and Lucretia, washing up noisily in the scullery, her door half open to insure the proprieties.

"Well?" asked Leslie.

"Very well—bewilderingly well."

"I told you about Mrs. Dawlish and what she intends to do?"

He nodded.

"You can, of course, charge her with being privy to the forgery, but I think it was Anita's work. It will be so much better if you allow her to pass the property to you by deed of gift. That makes you a very rich man, Peter. What are you going to do with it? Buy a house in Park Lane?"

"Would you like a house in Park Lane?" he asked.

"I'd like almost any kind of house, Peter," she said quietly.

Lucretia, looking through the half-opened door, saw the brown head of her mistress pillowed on Peter's shabby jacket, saw him bend his head and kiss her.

Lucretia sneered.

"My stars!" she said, addressing nobody in particular. "These women!"